Mel looked troubled in a way I had never seen before, as though once again she was forcing herself to review the details of a night she would rather forget. "We all got there—the early ones early, the late ones late—and we talked and helped in the kitchen and sat down later than expected. Just like any other year. Nothing at all was different."

I said nothing. I had no idea what was coming, what terrible event was about to transpire in her narrative.

"We ate the Passover meal the way we always did and I helped clear the table and then we all sat down again for the rest of the service. Grandma had a special cup, it was silver and very ornate, that we always used for Elijah, and Grandpa filled it and Aunt Iris said, 'I'll get the door,' and she got up and left. And what happened was, she never came back. . . ."

By Lee Harris
Published by Fawcett Books:

THE GOOD FRIDAY MURDER
THE YOM KIPPUR MURDER
THE CHRISTENING DAY MURDER
THE ST. PATRICK'S DAY MURDER
THE CHRISTMAS NIGHT MURDER
THE THANKSGIVING DAY MURDER
THE PASSOVER MURDER
THE VALENTINE'S DAY MURDER

THE PASSOVER MURDER

Lee Harris

FAWCETT GOLD MEDAL • NEW YORK

A Fawcett Gold Medal Book
Published by Ballantine Books
Copyright © 1996 by Lee Harris

All rights reserved under International and Pan-American Copyright Conventions. Published in the United States by Ballantine Books, a division of Random House, Inc., New York, and simultaneously in Canada by Random House of Canada Limited, Toronto.

http://www.randomhouse.com

Library of Congress Catalog Card Number: 95-90821

ISBN 0-449-14963-3

Manufactured in the United States of America

First Edition: April 1996

10 9 8 7 6 5 4

In memory of my Uncle Abram and Aunt Sonia
and for all the cousins in Toronto
who made the seders of my childhood so memorable.

Why is this night different
from all other nights?
　　　　—from the Passover Haggadah

The author wishes to thank
Ana M. Soler, James L. V. Wegman,
and Arthur Rich
for their help and priceless information.

1

"What I'm really trying to say," my friend Melanie Gross said over the telephone, "is that it's going to be a slightly crazy experience, but I think you'll enjoy it."

"I know I'll enjoy it. And if it's a little crazy, I'll enjoy it more."

"You're so easy to get along with, Chris. It's a relief after my family."

"For someone who takes on more than I could ever handle, you seem too worried about this, Mel. This is the third time you've talked about it."

"I guess you'll just have to see for yourself. See you tomorrow night."

Tomorrow night was the Passover seder, an event I had been only dimly aware of for most of the years of my life, fifteen of which had been spent in St. Stephen's Convent in upstate New York. But since my departure, since becoming a layperson for the first time in my adult life, my friendships and experiences had so expanded that at times I had felt nearly breathless. I had become a homeowner first, an amateur investigator into unsolved murders next, and rapidly after that had fallen in love and become good friends with people I would never have met had I remained in the convent. Mel was a Jewish neighbor, and now closest friend, who had taught me to bake Christmas cookies and helped me arrange the most beautiful wedding St. Stephen's had ever hosted. Now my husband, Jack, and I were to be guests at her seder.

For weeks I had seen the shelves in our local supermarket fill with tantalizing foods, some of which I could not even pronounce. There were special mixes for cakes, cans of macaroons, boxes of matzohs, jars of fish, packages of candies, all labeled "Kosher for Passover." When I bought myself a container of yogurt recently I noticed that it, too, was marked "Kosher for Passover." What did it all mean?

"Traditionally," Melanie explained as we sat sipping tea in her family room one cold afternoon, "all the food in the house is cleared out before Passover and replaced with new, special foods."

"You mean you throw out all your leftovers?"

"You throw out everything, not just the leftovers. If you have a can of soup you haven't used or a bottle of Scotch in the cupboard, that all goes out, too. Clean out the shelves, the refrigerator, the pantry, everything. Then you buy all new food that's kosher for Passover."

"How is it different?"

"Nothing is leavened," she said. "No flour, no rice, no corn. That's a reminder of the time in Egypt, when there wasn't any bread, just matzoh. It was baked in the open in the sun, and that's why it looks and feels the way it does. It's hard and crisp and thin and has an uneven surface." She showed me a piece. "So we remember that and we eat unleavened bread. And everything we use, the dishes, the pots, the eating utensils, are special for these days."

"You have another set of dishes and silver?" I asked.

"People who keep kosher have two, one for meat and one for dairy."

"But what about my yogurt? What makes that different? The label says the same things are in it."

"Once a year the company cleans out its equipment or buys new equipment and they use it first to make Passover foods. The milk is put in new bottles, not old ones, things like that."

"And when Passover is over you go back to the usual dishes and food?"

"Right. We can use up the Passover leftovers, but the dishes get packed away till next year."

"I had no idea it was such an extensive transformation. It's like a different way of living for a while."

"That's just what it is. And you'll get a taste of it at the seder."

"Can I help with anything?"

"Oh, thanks, no. My mother'll spend the day with me and we'll cook together. It's much easier nowadays because you can buy those foil bakers and throw them out when you're finished with them. In the old days, you had to keep a separate set of pans for the occasion."

"Tell me who's coming."

"Most of my crazy family."

"You always say that and they're the sanest people I've ever met."

"Keep an open mind," Mel said. "You may have to change it. Would you like to read a Haggadah before the seder?"

"What did you say?"

"The Haggadah. It's the special book we follow during the seder. It explains the seder."

"I'd love to see it in advance. At least I'll have some idea what's going on."

Mel shook her head. "You won't, but it won't be your fault. I don't know why it always works out this way, but we rarely use two Haggadahs that are the same. Every translation is different, and if you lose your place, you won't be alone. Some people will read in Hebrew, some people will read in English. One of my uncles will fall asleep and one of my aunts will start to cry and have to leave the table and two or three cousins will go with her and everyone will forget where they were."

"Is it such a sad occasion?"

"The seder? Sad? Oh, you mean because my aunt cries. No, it's not sad at all. It's really a very happy occasion, the deliverance from Egypt. The children are there and we sing and eat a lot. It's just that my aunt— well, it's a sad occasion for her. Something happened a long time ago. I really can't go into it. You know how it is; something happens around a holiday, and whenever that holiday comes, you think of it. I think you'll have a good time. My grandfather will love you and he'll talk your ear off, my mother's looking forward to seeing you again, and everyone else is reasonably nice."

"And slightly crazy."

She gave me a big smile. "You got it. Let me find you a Haggadah to give you something to do with your idle time."

Since I couldn't cook or bake anything to help Mel, and I don't know enough about wine to make a good choice, I decided to send flowers for her table. They arrived in the afternoon and I got an ecstatic phone call thanking me and saying how perfect they were. When the call came, I was sipping a cup of tea and reading the Haggadah Mel had given me. What I learned was that the ceremony was the story of the Exodus from Egypt, that the children ask questions and their father gives the answers, the answers being the story. While the narration was going on, the guests would drink four glasses of wine and eat the special foods Mel had told me about. Although the explanation was in English, there were transliterated words I could not pronounce, but I assumed I would get by. I was rather pleased to see that a description of the table included flowers. I was starting off on the right foot.

My one concern that afternoon was Jack. Jack is a detective sergeant with the NYPD and works out of the Sixty-fifth Precinct in Brooklyn. The previous day he had become involved in what looked like a major crime and he had worked late the night before and gone in early this morning. I knew better than to ask if he thought he would be home in time for the seder; if he could make it, he would. But when the phone rang at six, the time he would normally be leaving the station house, I sensed what the call would be about.

"You still love me?" his voice said when I answered.

"Passionately."

"And you're a very forgiving person, right?"

"You can't make it."

"It's iffy. What did Mel say, eight o'clock?"

"Seven-thirty to meet the family. She's adamant about sitting down at eight."

"I may get there for dessert."

"Don't push yourself, Jack. You know Mel will have plenty for you to eat even if you don't get there at all."

"The woman is an angel."

"How's it going?"

"This is a tough one and everything has to be a hundred and ten percent correct. I can already see myself on the witness stand next year."

"Take it easy driving home."

"Have a good time."

It's one of the things I've had to get used to, a schedule that's never as fixed as it looks on the chart. Other more normal people live by schedules or books; detectives live by charts. Even Jack's evening law school classes have suffered when he had to remain at a crime scene hours beyond his tour. It's a job he loves, and that's part of the price.

At seven-thirty I put my coat on and walked down the street to the Grosses' house. There were cars in the driveway and along the curb, and all the lights were on inside. Mel's mother, Marilyn Margulies, opened the door and wrapped her arms around me.

"Chris! You look marvelous. Come in, dear. What lovely flowers you sent. Where's Jack?"

Mrs. Margulies helped me select my wedding dress and handled a lot of details for my wedding, so I think of her as part of the family. She ushered me inside and introduced me to so many people that their names simply passed through my memory as I greeted them.

"And this is my father," Mrs. Margulies said with obvious pride, "Abraham Grodnik. Pop, this is Christine Bennett Brooks, Mel's friend from across the street. It's Chris's first seder."

He was old and thin—I guessed near ninety—and had a small beard trimmed to a neat point. He wore a dark blue suit with a vest and a small, round satin cap that Mel had told me was called a yarmulke. But what was most striking about him was his eyes, bright, intelligent, and very blue. He held out his hand, grasped mine more firmly than I expected, and said, "I am very pleased to make your acquaintance."

"Talk to her, Pop," Mrs. Margulies said. "I have to run back to the kitchen."

"You don't have to tell me," the old man called after his daughter. "I still remember how." He turned back to me as I sat beside him. "So this is your first seder?" He shifted on his chair to make himself more comfortable. "I don't remember my first one anymore. I was maybe three or four. It was a long time ago. We lived under the czar in those times. You know the czar?"

"I know the history, yes. When did you come to this country?"

"Nineteen-oh-seven," he said precisely. "With my parents, they should rest in peace, and my sister, she should rest in peace. The rest of them were born here, down in New York. You know the lower east side?"

"I've been there."

"A lot has changed. It's a place you come to first. Then, when life gets better, you go somewhere else. The Jews are gone and other poor people are there now. When they do better, they'll pick up and move, too. This place—" he looked around the large, comfortable room we were sitting in "—this beautiful house my granddaughter lives in, this is the place you come to last. My granddaughter and her husband are very rich to have a house like this."

"They're very nice people," I said, not anxious to discuss the economic status of my friends.

"You're right. Nice is more important than rich. Rich comes and goes. I have seen this. Nice is forever."

"I like the sound of that."

He smiled. "You like the sound of the words. Seventy-five, eighty years ago I knew in my heart I would be a poet. In my house I got a whole carton full of poems by Abraham Grodnik. You know what they're worth?"

"Probably a lot more than being rich."

He inspected my face before he responded. "You're a nice girl," he said. "My granddaughter got herself a nice girlfriend. So tell me, you know what this seder's all about?"

"I've been reading the book." I was a little afraid to say the Hebrew word aloud, but I showed it to him.

"The Haggadah, it's called. That one you have is a little different from the one I have, but we all get along here. You sit next to me. You have any questions, you ask me. By now, I know the whole thing by heart."

"I have one question before we start. Do I really have to drink four glasses of wine?"

"Nobody counts in this family. You drink what you want, you eat what you want. Here we tell the story and we have a good time."

I was about to say something when a young couple came over and greeted Mr. Grodnik effusively. I gathered they were grandchildren, or grandchild and spouse, and I was impressed that he knew their names and asked relevant questions about them. There was no doubt about the sharpness of his mind.

"This is Christine," he said after a minute, "Melanie's friend. Tonight is her first seder."

"Oh, I know who you are," the young woman said. "Mel's told me all about you. I'm her cousin Bobbie, and this is my husband, Miles. I'm so glad to meet you."

"Thank you. Same here."

"Just have a good time and eat a lot. Mel's food is the best."

"I know."

"Well, we'll leave you two. We have a lot of hellos to say."

"Hellos, good-byes, it's the story of life," Abraham Grodnik said. "They should take a little time between the beginning and the end and enjoy what's in the middle."

"You've enjoyed the middle," I said.

"A lot of it, when I could. It wasn't always easy. Today everything is easy; nothing is hard anymore. The bagels are full of air, the beds are soft. Nobody walks anymore. They got rid of the hard part. But for me the middle is over, Christine. This is my last seder."

I felt a chill pass through me. "What do you mean?"

"Next year this time I won't be around anymore."

"Are you ill?"

"Ill, failing, whatever you want to call it. I hope to see spring, that's all. I like to see the leaves come out on the trees. It's my favorite season."

"Mine, too," I said. "It's right around the corner. I'm sure you'll make it."

He nodded and smiled. "You have to be young to be sure. You get older, nothing is certain anymore." He looked at his watch. "Eight o'clock. I thought my granddaughter said we sit down at eight sharp. What good is a promise if you don't keep it?"

2

Everything I had been told turned out to be true. It was a fascinating evening even though I got lost frequently in the narration. My book said that the youngest child present would ask the four questions, but it turned out that every child present asked them, and when the last had taken his turn, I could practically repeat the Hebrew words myself. The gist of the questions was why tonight was different from all others, why a different kind of bread was eaten, why bitter herbs were eaten, why the herbs were dipped in salt water and something I could not pronounce, and why this special dinner was held. As the children recited, I glanced at the Haggadah of the man sitting next to me and saw that his English translation was not the same as mine and that his book started from the right and not from the left as mine did.

After the questions, Mr. Grodnik, who sat at the head of the table, began to read in Hebrew. I followed my translation, which was the explanation of why we celebrated tonight, how God had delivered the Jews from Egypt. The reading then passed from one guest to another on the other side of the table, some of them reading in Hebrew, others in English. It began with the questions four different kinds of sons might ask: a wise

11

son, a wicked one, a simple one, and one unable to ask anything. And then the story began, Jacob going down to sojourn in Egypt. Time passed, the Jews multiplied, and the Egyptians treated them badly, to the point where their male children were slain. It was a bloody description, which I read as the people around me chanted the story in the ancient language.

Finally, God retaliated against the Egyptians with ten plagues, the last of which was the slaying of Egyptians' firstborn sons. At the recitation of each of the plagues, wine was spilled to commemorate it.

"You know what's going on?" Mr. Grodnik asked, leaning toward me.

"Pretty much. At least I get the big picture."

"The big picture, that's good. That's all you need tonight. You want to read something when it comes around to you?"

"Sure," I said gamely. "As long as it's in English."

"When it's your turn, I'll show you where to read."

I read a short paragraph about the Paschal Lamb and how the Lord spared the houses of the children of Israel in Egypt by passing over them, giving me an understanding of the name of the holiday. Then we continued to the meaning of the matzoh and the bitter herbs.

During all of this, very little was eaten, and the children, who were sitting at a separate table, were getting restless. A couple of the mothers left our table and went to placate them. I glanced at my watch. It was almost nine and they were probably pretty hungry by then. I thought of Jack, who might not have eaten for many hours, and hoped he would get here in time for more than a dessert. And just as I began to feel some hunger pangs myself, we reached the point of eating what my Haggadah described as a festive meal.

It was more than festive; it was magnificent, as though Mel had considered everyone's tastes and desires and catered to all of them. It was a huge meal beginning with a wonderful soup, then continuing with turkey and beef, many vegetables, plenty of matzoh instead of bread, and side dishes I had never seen or heard of but which I tried and enjoyed.

"You know," Mr. Grodnik said after passing turkey to me, "among the Conservative and Orthodox, this seder is repeated tomorrow night."

"You do all this again?"

"Everything, all the prayers, all the food, all the songs."

"I know that some Jews celebrate holidays for two days, but I've never really understood why."

"Why is simple. A long time ago, when the Jews lived mostly in Europe, they weren't sure if the day they celebrated was the same as the day the holiday was celebrated in Israel, so they celebrated twice, just to be on the safe side. In Israel they celebrate one day because they know what day it is, and here, the Reform Jews celebrate one day because time isn't a secret anymore. But for the Conservatives and the Orthodox, it's part of the way they practice."

"What do you do?"

"At my age, I do what the family wants. I have a son that does it two days, a daughter that does it one day. Tomorrow night I go to my son's house, I see some other parts of the family, I have another seder. It makes it easy when you have a big family; you don't have to see them all at once."

I sensed he was only half joking. In my life there is no difficulty with having too many relatives; I have practically none at all, having been an only child orphaned at fourteen. My only living relative now is my cousin Gene, who lives nearby in a residence for retarded adults. Besides being his guardian, I am very close to him and always have been. He's the person responsible for my nickname, Kix, a corruption of Chris when we were very young. And it is his mother's house that I inherited and now live in, his mother having been my father's sister. But they are all gone now, and it pleased me to look around the table and see all these people related by blood and marriage, all happy and eager to come together to share a holiday. It made me feel once again that I would like to continue the families that Jack and I come from, that I was already a couple of years into my thirties, and the time to do so might well be now.

When the meal was over the service continued and eventually the cups were filled for the fourth time, although I had barely drunk one full glass of wine.

Hal, Mel's husband, stood and said, "I'll get the door," and as he walked away, a woman at the other end of the table gasped.

Mr. Grodnik put his hand on my arm. "Don't worry about anything," he said, as though there were something to worry about. "Hal is opening the door now for Elijah, and we pour a glass of wine for him."

"Here's another glass, Grandpa," Mel said, bringing one over. "How's it going, Chris?"

"I'm eating it up."

"That's the best way. This glass is for Elijah." She set it on the table in front of Mr. Grodnik.

"The prophet?"

"That's right. All over the world, Jews are opening their doors for him and pouring him a glass of wine."

"Have you ever seen him?" I asked.

"Not so far, but it doesn't mean he's not here."

Hal had returned to the table and the reading continued, but the table had thinned out. One young woman was carrying her child on her shoulder, the child fast asleep. Others seemed to have left also, probably with their young, sleepy offspring. And from somewhere off to my right, I could hear the sound of weeping.

There was a slight stir, a woman on one side of the table and a man on the other pushing back their chairs and hurrying to the weeping woman. Mr. Grodnik's hand tightened on my forearm as though he were watching a play that he had seen before and he knew exactly what scene was coming up, exactly what the next move would be. The weeping woman was helped to her feet, and the three of them left the table and walked out of the room. A kind of sigh of relief settled over the remaining guests. People looked at each other, but nothing was said. Mr. Grodnik looked down at his Haggadah and then up at the table. Just as he began to chant, a very clear child's voice called out, "Are you Elijah?"

I turned along with everyone else toward the doorway to the dining room where my husband, Jack, had just made a spectacular entrance.

After the crowd, the house seemed almost too empty. Mel's children were up in bed, everyone but Jack and me was gone, and Mel and I were getting the dishes into the dishwasher.

"Your flowers were so perfect, Chris. I've never had an arrangement like that where it kind of crept down the table."

"It was a beautiful table. Everything was wonderful. And your little nephew will never forget that he went to the seder that Elijah visited."

"That was too much. Jack couldn't have timed it better if he'd had a stopwatch. I hate to say it because it's mean of me, but I'm almost glad he came late."

"You made up for it. He was starving when he walked in, but I don't think he'll eat again till tomorrow night."

"How'd you like that compote?"

"I've never had anything like it. What's in it?"

"Just apples and bananas and pineapple and cherries and cinnamon and sugar and orange juice and a little Grand Marnier."

"Just?" I laughed. "When I say 'just' it's followed by one paltry item."

"A little poetic license."

"Your grandfather told me he wanted to be a poet."

"He's quite a guy, isn't he? I knew you'd get along. If he'd been born fifty years later, he would have been a man of letters, maybe even a great poet. But when he came to this country, he had to work as soon as he was old enough. He has a wonderful mind and he's kept it fresh and open."

"Is he well?" I asked.

Her face changed. "Why do you ask?"

"Something he said. Maybe I misheard him." I said it because she looked both shocked and distressed.

"I'll have to check with Mom. My grandmother died several years ago, and the family's kept pretty close tabs on him since. I know he's thin, but I thought he was in good health."

"Your mother looked wonderful as usual," I said, to change the subject.

"Yes." Melanie's thoughts were clearly still on her grandfather. "What did he say to you?"

"He felt he was failing."

"Well, I can tell you he isn't. He's just fine and he's all there." She smiled. "Aren't you going to ask me about the great scene?"

"You mean your aunt? You told me it would happen. It was just exactly the way you said it would be."

"Aren't you curious? The first time Hal saw it, he asked me a hundred questions."

"I assume something sad happened at this season and she was just remembering it."

"It was more than just sad," Mel said, turning off the faucet finally and wiping her hands on a towel. "It was ghastly and horrifying. Come. We'll sit in the living room. It'll be nice and quiet and you can have a drink or a cup of coffee or anything that pleases you."

"A glass of your fizzy water," I said. I was late coming to the bottled water scene. To me it was still something special.

"Me, too," Mel said. She got a bottle out of the refrigerator, put some ice in two glasses, and we went into the living room and sat in two comfortable chairs. "That feels good," Mel said. "I should have put sneakers on after everyone left." She pulled a shoe off. "Ouch. Cooking is hard on the back and the feet."

"It was lovely, Mel."

"I was there the night it happened," she said. She had drunk half her water and put the glass down on a coaster. "It was a long time ago, maybe sixteen years. I was in college at the time and I flew home for the seder. Grandpa made a big fuss over me, I remember. He was pleased I was going to college and really happy that I had come home. My grandmother was alive and we all went to their apartment for the seder, which we did every year. My grandmother was an unbelievable cook, an instinctive cook. She could taste something in the pot and know exactly what it needed." She stopped, the memory overwhelming her.

"My grandfather had a lot of brothers and sisters; I don't really know how many there were because some died in infancy or childhood. Some were born in Russia, some here. The last one was Iris and she was much younger than Grandpa, fifteen years maybe, maybe even more. She was very pretty, petite, she laughed a lot, she loved the kids, she had a wonderful personality. We all adored her. But she never married, and I never really understood why. Men loved her. She was a natural flirt. She could walk in a room and every man would stop what he was doing and look at her. I used to hear that Aunt Iris was going out with this one or that one, but nothing ever lasted. At least, that's what I heard.

"Anyway, she was always at Grandma's seder along with everyone else, and she was there that night. More water?"

The offer jarred me. "No, thanks. Go on."

"As you can imagine, I've thought about it a lot since that night. And I can't remember one thing that was different or unusual or new about that night. The usual people were there, the usual food was served; everything was the way it always was. We were all much younger, but that goes without saying." She looked troubled in a way I had never seen before, as though once again she was forcing herself to review the details of a night she would rather forget. "We all got there—the early ones early, the late ones late—and we talked and helped in the kitchen and sat down later than expected. Just like every year. Nothing at all was different."

I said nothing. I had no idea what was coming, what terrible event was about to transpire in her narrative.

"We ate the Passover meal the way we always did, and I helped clear the table, and then we all sat down again for the rest of the service. Grandma had a special cup, it was silver and very ornate, that we always used for Elijah, and Grandpa filled it and Aunt Iris said, 'I'll get the door,' and she got up and left. And what happened was, she never came back."

"She walked out the door and disappeared?"

"When she didn't come back to the table, we called her and then we went looking for her, and when we realized she just wasn't in the apartment, Grandpa said, 'Call the police,' and we did."

"Did they come?"

"Right away. I guess whoever called—it must have been my father—said she'd been grabbed and taken away. That wasn't true—or at least, I don't think it was true—but that got them there fast."

"How do you know it wasn't true?"

Mel took a deep breath. "Because one of the cops asked what color coat Aunt Iris was wearing, and when we looked for it in the closet, it wasn't there. And her purse was gone, too."

"So you think she took the opportunity to run away."

"It really looked that way. I remember she was eager to open the door. I can still hear her saying, 'I'll get the door.' And then she jumped up and left the table."

"I suppose you couldn't see the door from where you were sitting."

"It was an old building and the apartments were laid out in such a way that there was no view of the door. It was around a corner and she had a bit of a walk to the door."

"Where was the coat closet?" I asked, interested in this story in spite of myself.

"Near the door to the apartment. She could have grabbed her coat and run out of the house, and no one would know it until she didn't come back. And don't bother asking about her purse. I have no idea where she put it, but most of the women left their bags in the foyer, either on the floor or on the little table. I couldn't even tell you if she carried one with her that night, but she must have. How could she have left home without one?"

"Is there more, Mel?"

"Oh, yes, there's more. What happened was—and I'm leaving out the misery the whole family lived through for the next forty-eight hours—what happened was that about two days later her body was found in a fenced-in area in a place she would never have gone to either alone or in company. She was wearing her coat, so we know she put it on before she left the apartment. I think one shoe was missing, and of course, her purse wasn't there. I had gone back to school by the time they found her, so I heard this from my mother, who's probably a better source than I am. I don't know what else I can tell you, but now you know why my aunt Sylvie breaks down every Passover and has to be taken away from the table. She was very close to Iris and she's a very emotional and sentimental person."

"Mel, you've never said whether they found the killer."

"They didn't. That's the long and short of it."

"Did the purse turn up?"

"I'm not sure, but I think the wallet did. My mother would remember."

"And your grandfather?"

"He remembers everything. If my grandmother were alive, she would, too."

"So the case is still open," I said.

"If open means unsolved, I guess it's still open. If they ever arrest someone and he admits he killed Aunt Iris, then we'll know who it is. But that's not going to happen sixteen years later, is it? He's probably dead by now."

"But, Mel, it had to be someone she knew."

"Because she took her coat and purse?"

"Yes. It means she went outside to meet someone. Don't you agree?"

Mel smiled. "It's your suspicious, investigative nature, Chris. Maybe she was hot and decided to run downstairs for a breath of fresh air."

"Without telling anyone?"

"She wasn't a child. Would you announce that you were going out if you intended to come right back?"

I thought about it and I wasn't sure of the answer.

"You girls talking up a storm?" Hal was standing at the entrance to the living room with Jack beside him.

I looked at my watch. "I think it all just ended, Hal. It's been a wonderful evening."

Five minutes later we were on our way.

3

A couple of weeks went by, and although I thought about Mel's story once or twice, I was too busy with other things to be concerned about it. My friend Arnold Gold, a lawyer for whom I work on an as-needed basis, had lots of work for me, and I continued teaching the poetry course that I began the September after I left St. Stephen's. I saw Mel as I often do during our morning walks, but neither of us mentioned Aunt Iris. It was as though she had gotten it off her chest and was done with it, although I knew it was the sort of event that no one is ever really done with, least of all those close to the victim.

When Jack and I had gotten home the night of the seder, he had been so tired we had just gone to bed, and I had not mentioned Mel's story. Later, when he was out from under the big case he had been working on, he found he had accumulated a lot of time he could take as vacation and he boldly suggested we go away for a weekend, and I equally boldly said I thought it would be a terrific idea. So we hopped into the car early one morning and drove to Washington, D.C., my first trip there and a memorable one. The weather was mild, the trees were in bloom, and we visited one wonderful place after another and took a lot of pictures.

I felt happy and refreshed when we returned, looking forward to digging in the garden now that spring was really here and the days were longer. On the Wednesday after our return, I put on a heavy sweater, left Jack to make breakfast, and went out the side door and down the driveway to the street. Turning left as I always did, I loped along at a comfortable pace toward the Grosses' house. Sure enough, their side door opened just as I approached, and Mel jogged down the driveway toward the street.

"How was Washington?" she called, joining me.

"Wonderful. Relaxing, interesting, beautiful. I'll show you the pictures when I get them developed. It was a great vacation. You should take the family down there."

"We will. We just want to wait till the kids are big enough so that they won't demand to be picked up when they get tired. Maybe next year."

"We're going to have nice green leaves soon, Mel. I can't wait."

"And nice black earth to turn over. I can almost smell it. You working today?"

"I have stuff for Arnold, but I'm doing it at home. I'll get started as soon as Jack leaves, and I should be done by early afternoon."

"How about a little kaffeeklatsching at three?"

"Sounds good. Anything up?"

"I just feel like talking."

"Me, too. I'll see you at three."

* * *

I wrapped up my work before one, had some soup for lunch, and drove to the post office to get the material in the mail for Arnold. That gave me a little time to shop at the supermarket and get to Mel's house by three. I could smell the coffee as I stepped inside, and a coffee cake on her kitchen counter assured me she had been busy and I was in for a treat. Mel does all these things with the ease of a professional. Before I bake, I make lists, check my pantry, and figure out how much time is needed and how much time I have. I keep hoping that her self-assurance will rub off on me, but I don't think I'll ever achieve her complete offhandedness when it comes to baking.

"Get your work done?" she asked as we carried things into the family room.

"Everything. Printed, posted, on its way."

"Arnold's lucky to have you."

"And vice versa. For a man with a very cynical view of a large part of life, he's the kindest, most thoughtful employer in the world."

"I have some terrible news, Chris," Mel said.

"Mel, what happened?"

"What you said about my grandfather, it's true. I asked Mom after the seder, and she had a heart-to-heart with Grandpa. He has a malignancy and they're not going to treat it, partly because of his age and condition and partly because he put his foot down and said he didn't want it."

"I'm so sorry. Your Passover seder will never be the same again."

"Nothing will ever be the same. I can't imagine the family without that man at the head. I just heard the news over the weekend and I can't stop thinking about it. He's always been there. I keep wondering if we'll still be a family without him."

"You will. You have a very solid family. Everyone there that night wanted to be there. They weren't just doing it to please your grandfather."

"You're right. We all get along. There's some back-biting, but down deep, we all pull together."

"Your mother must be very upset."

"She is. She spoke to his doctor yesterday and confirmed everything. She was really hoping—" Mel stopped. "But there isn't anything they can do. It's just a matter of time."

I decided not to utter a platitude. She knew far better than I what a great man her grandfather was, how he would be missed, how strong he had been and how strong he continued to be. Saying it would neither help nor comfort her. "I'm glad I had the chance to meet him," I said. "Even more, I'm glad I had a chance to sit next to him during the seder."

"Yes." She smiled. "So am I. You're another person who'll remember him." She drank some coffee and looked as sad as I knew she felt. "Chris, Mom and I did a lot of talking over the weekend. I told her you and I had discussed Aunt Iris. We want you to do something for us."

I knew what was coming as though I had written the script myself. "No, Mel," I said firmly. "I can't. I would do anything for you, you know that. I will help you nurse your grandfather if you need me. I'll watch your kids while you go to see him. But I can't do what you're about to ask me to do."

"But you're the perfect person. You're not part of the family, but you've met us all. You can keep a secret so if someone tells you something, it won't go any further. And you have the background and the common sense to know where to look and what questions to ask. Grandpa deserves to know what happened to his youngest sister. There isn't much time left and the police have failed. If there's an answer, Mom and I think you can find it."

"Did it ever occur to you that your grandfather might not want to know what happened?"

"What do you mean?"

"I mean suppose it's something sordid and ugly. Shouldn't something like that stay unknown?"

"Aunt Iris? Sordid and ugly? It's not possible."

"Mel, you're talking like the seventeen-year-old you were when it happened. You're in your thirties now. Think about it. She was a single woman in her fifties. She dated, she was a natural flirt—these are all things you told me that night. She wasn't a mousy little girl who clung to her parents and never left home. She lived by herself, she had a private life she may not have shared with her family. You were a kid, Mel. You had no idea what kind of life she led when she wasn't being your adoring aunt. You don't know who her friends were, how she spent her free time, who she spent it with."

"You're right. I don't know."

"And you don't want to know. Why don't you just leave it as it is? Your beloved aunt went out for a breath of fresh air, and someone trying to rob her ended up killing her. That's probably what the truth is, and if it is, I can't do anything the police haven't already done."

"I never thought of it that way," Mel said, "about her having a life outside the family, but you're right. The only time I saw her was in a family setting except maybe if she took me to the zoo when I was little. But I was never part of a group that included her friends. I only met one of them in my whole life, but there must have been others. What you're suggesting—"

"I'm not suggesting anything," I said. "I'm saying that as a child, as a teenager, there's so much about the older members of the family that you didn't know." I was speaking from a fairly new experience of my own. "One generation keeps secrets from the next generation. So you see why I can't investigate and why it's really better to leave it alone."

Mel got up and went to a shelf in the bookcase that filled one wall of the family room. She took down an album, opened it, and flipped several pages. "I can't leave it alone," she said. "This is a picture of Aunt Iris and me when I graduated from high school."

There was Mel's familiar sweet face with her marvelous, encompassing smile. Beside her was a shorter, slim woman with a strong family resemblance. She was dressed beautifully for the occasion in a pale peach suit that could have been linen, a strand of pearls sitting at her throat, an elegant bag in one hand. Her grandniece looked almost tall by comparison in her white academic robe and mortarboard.

"She's very pretty," I said. "You look like that side of the family, don't you?"

"Except I'll never be as slim as Iris. I think she had magic hormones or got all the good genes. Look at that waist. I wasn't that thin when I was ten."

"She's lovely. What kind of work did she do?"

"She was a secretary, the kind a boss couldn't live without. She used to get terrific bonuses at the end of the year. She probably spent all of it on my cousins and me."

"You have such wonderful memories," I said.

"Chris, I have got to know." She took the album, looked at the picture, turned a page and looked at some more before closing it. "If she went out for fresh air and was killed by one of those nameless monsters that commit random violence, so be it, but I think there's another explanation. I think she went out to help someone she knew, maybe someone who lived near my grandparents, and something happened—maybe an argument—and he killed her."

"Why do you think that?" I asked.

"Because she was a good person and she was generous. Maybe someone at work asked her for a loan, a hundred dollars, and Iris said, 'Meet me tonight at eleven o'clock in front of my brother's apartment house and I'll give it to you.' I think that's what happened."

"Then why did this person kill her?"

"He wanted more," Mel said with fervor. "A lot more. He looked at how she was dressed and he guessed she had a lot of money. He made demands and she turned him down and he—or she—I don't know. These things happen. People have tempers and the wrong word sets them off. The other is too easy, that someone walked down the block at the exact moment she went outside, that he robbed her and then killed her. Why did he kill her if he had her money? And how can you explain how he got her body half a dozen miles away from Grandpa's? How many muggers do you know that come equipped with their own cars?"

"OK, I agree it wasn't a simple mugging."

"Chris, once you agree with that, I've got you."

I laughed. "Is all this about tripping me up?"

Mel smiled and relaxed. "You bet, and now I've done it and you owe me. Look. Mom and I put our heads together over the weekend and we came up with all the names and addresses you need to begin. Not only that, but my car and I are available to bring people to your doorstep so you don't have to run around yourself. Am I making it appealing?" she asked in an almost plaintive voice.

It was appealing. If Mel had been a stranger, I would have been sorely tempted. I didn't believe any more than she did that her great-aunt had gone out for a walk and been robbed and murdered. It was even possible that some member of the family knew things about Iris that he had not admitted to the police for the reason I had brought up a little while ago, that there was a sordid, ugly side to her life. I didn't want to be the person to uncover such information. I thought Abraham Grodnik, in particular, would die a happier man if he didn't know the details of his youngest sister's life and death. But here, on my lap, were sheets of paper with names and addresses on them, Mr. Grodnik's at the top, Marilyn Margulies's next, Aunt Sylvie's near the bottom. There was a list of people who had been at the Passover seder the night Aunt Iris walked out the door, never to be seen again alive. There was even a sketch of the apartment showing how impossible it would have been for anyone to have seen Aunt Iris after she left the table.

"You've done a lot of work," I said.

"Because we care. Nobody cares as much as a family does. All due respect to Jack and the police department, but when they've looked in the usual places and talked to the usual suspects, there isn't much motivation for them to continue. I think someone killed Aunt Iris intentionally or because he became enraged with her, someone who knew her, someone she trusted, someone she made an appointment to see that night. Even after all these years, he shouldn't get away with it."

I agreed with everything she said, but I still didn't want to be the one to ask the difficult questions and come up with the awful answers. And yet it tugged at me, the memory of the snapshot, the beautiful smiling woman who was so good to those who loved her.

"Did she drive?" I asked.

"I don't know." Mel looked distressed. "It's terrible, Chris. You ask these perfectly reasonable, simple questions about a woman I knew from the day I was born, and I can't answer them. I never saw her drive. When we went somewhere together, we always took the subway or a bus or sometimes a taxi. But that doesn't mean she didn't know how to drive. I just don't know."

"Where did she live?"

"When I was young, she had an apartment in the Bronx on the Grand Concourse, but a few years before she died, she decided it wasn't a safe place to live anymore, especially if she came home at night by herself, and she went out a lot to concerts and the theater and lectures. So she moved to Manhattan. It was a small apartment in a good building and it was very nice and she furnished it beautifully. I used to love to go there."

"Did she leave a will?"

"Yes. My cousins and I inherited her money. My parents put it away for me."

"Mel, I really think—"

"Don't say it." Mel stood and came over to my chair.

"Take the papers with you. Think about it. Think about
the seder, about someone saying it was time to open the
door for Elijah and this eager voice pipes up, 'I'll get
the door.' Listen to it in your head. 'I'll get the door.'
And then watch this small, lovely woman leave the table, walk out of the room, and never look back."

I told her I would think about it and I went home.

4

Eventually it was too intriguing and too easy to begin for me to turn it down. The fact that the murder had occurred so long ago also made it easier to accept. The family knew that Iris Grodnik was dead; they knew how she had been murdered. Nothing would bring her back. All they could possibly hope to gain from an investigation was answers.

I called Mel the next morning and said, "I need some information before I can seriously look into your aunt's murder."

"Anything, Chris. Mom and I will find out whatever you want."

"I want the name of Iris's friend, the one you said you met. And I'd like the name of the company she worked for and also the man."

"He's dead. I saw his obituary in the *Times* several years ago."

"Well, see if you can come up with his name anyway. It's so long ago, I expect no one's left that remembers her. Did this friend of hers work at the same place?"

"I don't think so. I think they were friends from childhood or high school. They went way back."

"Was the friend married?"

"I couldn't tell you. It's possible."

"I guess you wouldn't know if she's alive," I said hopefully.

"No idea. But if she was Iris's age, which she should have been, she'd be about seventy-five now, give or take."

"Well, lots of people live to seventy-five these days, so let's hope." I looked down at the notes I had made last night while waiting for Jack to get home from law school. "The friend is the one I really want to talk to. She knew Iris well and she's not part of the family. Her perceptions will be different; her interests won't be the same as the family's."

"I'll do my best."

"The other one I want to talk to is your aunt Sylvie. Is she in good health?"

"Well, she's old, in her eighties, but I don't know that she's in poor health."

"Because I don't want to bring on heart attacks when I ask questions. It isn't worth it. The living have top priority."

"I agree. If I hear of anything, I'll let you know."

"If it's all right with both of you, I'd like to start with your mother, because you and she are the moving force here."

"Sure it's all right with me. I'll call Mom as soon as I get off the phone and see what I can arrange. If she's not tied up, I'll get her out here this afternoon."

"Whatever's convenient for her, Mel. There's no rush. All we're trying to do here is lay some ghosts to rest."

"OK. Anything else?"

"Yes, something very important. Someone will have

to give me the address where the body was found. That's the precinct that handled the homicide, and it's just possible that the detectives on the case are still around."

"Mom may remember. I went back to school before she was found, and almost everything I know after the seder is what my mother told me."

"OK. I have straightening up to do. Give me a call when you've got something."

"You bet."

It goes without saying that Jack thought I was crazy. But like the good detective he is, his interest was piqued by the story, especially since it was an NYPD case. There would be a file on it that would tell me who had been interviewed, what the medical findings were, what suspects, if any, had been questioned. While the family's recollections may have changed over the years, the documents in the file would not. Cross-checking would let me know who was most believable, if stories varied from one family member to another.

But I wanted to start with Marilyn Margulies because she was willing and eager and because I liked and trusted her. I didn't have long to wait. Mel called back so soon after our conversation that I had scarcely begun my cleanup.

"Chris? You available for lunch? Mom's ready."

"Lunch sounds great. Give me a time and I'll be there."

"Let's say twelve-thirty. I have to run out and shop and throw something together."

"I'll be there."

"Don't dress. I know Mom is a bit intimidating, but keep your jeans on."

I laughed. "I don't think of her as intimidating, but she does always look as though she's on her way to somewhere special."

"She is. Anywhere she goes is special. That's how she looks at life."

I thought it was a pretty good way to look at life, but I agreed to keep my jeans on. But just because I thought Marilyn Margulies was pretty special, I put on a new cotton knit sweater from my favorite catalog before locking up the house and walking down the street.

"How did you like our seder?" Mrs. Margulies said after we had kissed.

"It was wonderful, especially since Jack was mistaken for Elijah."

"Well, we're not likely to forget that very soon. Come, let's have lunch so we can start our conversation."

We went into the kitchen, where Mel had made the table look festive. She had platters with salads, slices of smoked salmon, and some wonderful breads. Linen napkins and crystal wineglasses made it look like the feast I knew it would be.

"Wine, Mel?" I said. "I'll fall asleep taking notes."

"You always threaten, but you never do. A glass won't hurt, and Hal just bought a case of this. It's a burgundy and he thinks it's wonderful. Sit down."

We did and she poured. "Marvelous," her mother said. "Oh, Mel, this is wonderful. Tell Hal to get a case for us. Daddy will love it."

I had to admit that I liked it myself, my palate, dormant for so many years, finally awakening to the good tastes in life. We spent a pleasant half hour eating and talking about ourselves and our families, leaving the topic of the day for later. Finally, a little after one, we retired to the family room to begin.

"I'd like to ask you about your father," I said, settling in a chair.

"What can I say? There's nothing good, but he's bearing up very well. He's known about this for a while, but he didn't want to worry us. That's the way he's always been."

"Where does he live?" I asked.

"With my sister in New York. I invited him to move in with us years ago, but he said he liked the city, that he was a city boy and he didn't want to live in the country. My sister lives in an apartment in Manhattan, and that gives him the chance to walk in the city. But he's never given up the old apartment, the one we all grew up in. And now he says he wants to go back and die there."

"Is it still furnished?"

"It's pretty much the way he left it a couple of years ago. The furniture is all there, my mother's china, the old seventy-eight records, the rugs. I don't want him to go back, but if he insists, we'll have to go along with it. He's likely to walk out of my sister's apartment one day and take a taxi home. That's the way he is."

I didn't blame him and I told her so. Then I took out my notebook and turned to a fresh page. "Tell me what you remember of Iris, from as far back as you can."

"Well." Mrs. Margulies gave me a small smile and sat back. She was wearing a two-piece knit dress in a fine black wool with a little white around the hem of the skirt, the round neckline, and the edge of the sleeves. Several thin gold chains hung around her neck, and I could see gold on her right wrist and on several fingers. Some of the rings, I recalled, were antique and very beautiful, with the kind of work one doesn't see much nowadays. By contrast, her daughter and I wore wedding rings and little other jewelry.

"I think she was always everyone's favorite aunt," she said. "She wasn't more than twenty years older than I and she lived with my grandparents—that's my father's parents—when I was growing up. So whenever I went to see my grandparents, I would see Aunt Iris. The others were gone. They were older, they got married, they moved out. But Iris stayed for a long time. I think she must have been in her thirties before she left home."

"Was there a problem when she left?"

"These are things I wouldn't know," Marilyn Margulies said. "My father would know because he was her brother. I have to tell you I come from a family that felt it wasn't proper to tell children stories about the older generation, and that continues to this day. I'm sure my father knows gossip about people who are long gone, but he would never tell me because I'm a child."

"I know about things like that, Mrs. Margulies. My own family also kept secrets in much the same way."

"Chris." She leaned forward in her chair. "You must call me Marilyn."

"OK." I smiled. It would make things easier, and I was happy to be part of her circle of friends. "So she left at some point and got her own apartment. Did she have a roommate?"

"Oh, I don't think she ever lived with anyone. She

didn't have to. She could afford her own place, and I think she liked keeping house. My grandmother helped her when she got started. I know this because when Aunt Iris died, many of my grandmother's things were in Iris's apartment."

"Then your grandparents probably weren't upset that a single daughter left home before she married."

"I don't think so. And if they were, they came around."

"Tell me about her work."

"She was the world's greatest secretary. She worked for one man for years and years. It wasn't her first job, but it was her longest and the last one. She was always there when he needed her and he was good to her. I think he once paid her way to Europe for a vacation."

"Do you think there was anything romantic between them?" I asked.

"You mean like an affair? No, I wouldn't think so."

"Why not?"

"Because—well, Iris wouldn't do that. I'm sure she kept her social life separate from her work."

I was somewhat amused at Marilyn's instant shooting down of my little balloon. It was pretty clear that she had no idea what Iris's social life was all about, if she had one, but the thought of her aunt engaged in something illicit was too repugnant to consider.

"What was her social life like?" I asked, since the matter was on the table.

"Well, she spent a lot of time with her family and she had a good friend from childhood that she saw a lot of."

"Did she date?"

"I think so."

"Did you ever meet anyone she went out with?"

"There was one man—what was his name? He used to visit her at her apartment and sometimes he came to my grandparents'. Mr., Mr. . . . If I think of the name, I'll let you know."

"He was the only one?"

"The only one I ever met, but I'm sure she went out."

"What about this old friend? Do you remember her at all?"

"Oh yes. Her name was Shirley, Shirley Finster, I think. I used to see her a lot. Do you remember her, Melanie?"

"I met her a couple of times. But only when I was a child. By the time I was in my teens, I don't remember seeing her anymore."

"You know, you're right. I wonder if anything happened or maybe Shirley just moved away. Maybe she got married and moved out of the city."

"Do you remember seeing her at Iris's funeral?" I asked.

"Mm. That's a good question. And I don't remember."

"Were you at the funeral?" I asked Mel.

She shook her head. "Mom didn't want me to come. She was afraid it would upset me. I stayed at school."

"It would have been too much for her," Marilyn said. "Just living through that terrible night when Iris walked out was bad enough."

"Tell me about that night," I said.

"The seder," she said reflectively, taking a deep breath. "It was as usual as every seder I've ever attended, which means a lot of things happened that were typical of my family and probably don't happen in anyone else's family."

"Like what?"

"Like the usual squabbles about who would sit where. We never had enough room at the big table for everyone, so we put the children at a separate table in another room. Sometimes the older ones didn't want to sit with the younger ones and sometimes the little ones wanted to be with their parents and we would play a kind of musical chairs until we had everything settled. Then there were always the latecomers and my father would get angry because we wanted to start on time, and I don't think we ever started on time in my whole life."

"I remember your father looking at his watch at eight and saying he'd been promised an eight-o'clock start."

"See?" Marilyn said. "Nothing changes. And although I can't really tell you what happened and what didn't happen that night, I'm sure most of those things went on and Pop got angry because we were late and someone probably showed up fifteen minutes after we got started and made Pop angry all over again."

"Uncle Dave was late," Mel said. "I remember. Grandpa was furious."

"Uncle Dave is always late. He's never learned how to be on time in his life. And he never will."

"What about Iris?" I asked.

"Oh, Iris was there early. She was helping Mom in the kitchen."

"Were you there when she arrived?"

"I don't think so," Marilyn said. "I think she was probably there most of the afternoon and I came later."

"So you didn't see her hang up her coat or put her pocketbook down."

"No. I'm sure she was there when I came."

"Do you remember what she was wearing?"

"Not really. I think she had an apron on when I got there and I just didn't notice later when she took it off. But I can tell you she always dressed well, and for a seder she would have worn something very nice, probably new. She was a beautiful woman, tiny, perfect figure; clothes looked like they were made for her."

"How did she act that night?"

"The same. It's hard to separate out that seder from all the others, but you can believe that after she disappeared, we all gave that night a lot of scrutiny, and I couldn't remember anything that seemed different or unusual. I told that to the police. Do you remember how our seder began, Chris? With the four questions?"

"I remember very well. All the children asked them."

"The first question is: 'Wherefore is this night different from all other nights?' I must have asked myself that question a thousand times in the weeks and months that followed. What was different about that night? What was different about Iris? What was different about the people at the table? And the answer was always nothing. It was the same as the year before and the year before that. What was different was that Iris walked out of the apartment when she opened the door for Elijah."

"Do you remember her leaving the table?"

"Yes, I remember. I was sitting near her, not right next to her, maybe two seats down. And somebody said, 'It's time for Elijah,' and Iris said, 'I'll go.' And she pushed her chair back from the table and walked out of the room."

"How long did it take for people to notice that she hadn't come back?"

"It took a while," Marilyn said. "We just continued with the Haggadah. I don't think anyone really noticed she wasn't there. People get up and sit down all the time. I know when it happened," she said as if she had just remembered. "The reading went around the table and then it was her turn and her seat was empty. Mom called her. Then maybe my brother did. Then maybe I got up to look for her. Nobody was in the bathroom. The bedrooms were empty. Only the children were at the children's table. So I went to the front door. It was still open just a crack. No one was in the kitchen. I closed the front door and went back to the table and I said I couldn't find her. I didn't think for a moment she had left the apartment. I just thought she was somewhere and I didn't know where."

"Do you remember what happened then?"

"I think everyone started calling and looking for her. Pop was furious. He wanted to continue the reading. But Mom was a little nervous. And then Aunt Sylvie started to cry. Do you remember Sylvie?"

"I remember."

"She's a very delicate little woman, very emotional. Her husband died years ago, but she can't talk about him without getting teary. Not that I blame her. He was a wonderful man and he was very good to her. But when she started to cry, I felt scared."

"How long did you look for her?"

"I don't know, another five minutes, maybe."

"Did anyone go outside to look for her?"

"Not right away. Who would imagine she would leave in the middle of the seder?"

"Do you remember who the first person was that suggested it?"

"No. All of a sudden it seemed to occur to all of us at once. My brother put his coat on and went out to look for her, and we kept looking around the apartment like crazy people, looking under beds, looking in closets. And then my father said, 'Call the police.' "

"How long do you think it was from the time Iris left the table till the police were called?"

"A long time," Marilyn said. "Fifteen minutes, anyway. Maybe more. It's because no one noticed she wasn't at the table for so long."

"What happened when the police came?"

"It was chaos. My husband had called and he told them over the phone that Aunt Iris had been grabbed by a man in the hall, which wasn't true, but he wanted them there right away and it worked. Two officers came, they talked to us, they asked us some questions, and then one of them said, 'What color coat was she wearing?' And that was the first time we thought to look for her coat in the closet. It wasn't there."

"I can imagine what the officers said."

"They said that she probably went out for a breath of fresh air. By that time, they had pretty much straightened out the story and they were angry that my husband had lied to them over the phone. They said we should call her at home, that she'd probably be there soon, and let them know what happened."

"You said your brother went looking for her."

"He walked around the block, and when he came back, he saw the police car and came upstairs."

"And you called Iris's number."

"A hundred times. In the morning my brother called

the police and said she hadn't been seen all night. They don't investigate right away, you know."

"I know."

"By the time they were ready to get started, someone found her body."

"How long had she been dead?"

"Long enough that they were pretty sure she'd been killed on the first night of Passover."

"So all your fears were well founded," I said.

"All our fears, the ones we admitted to and the others, the ones we couldn't bring ourselves to think."

"What was she wearing when they found her?"

"Her coat," she said, as though that were the important thing. "She was wearing her new winter coat."

"Were there signs of sexual abuse?"

"None."

"What about jewelry?"

"Now I have to think. What I remember is that she was wearing a gold ring, but I think everything else was gone, her watch, her bracelet, whatever she was wearing on her dress."

"And her purse?"

"It was never found."

"Mom," Mel said, "I thought they found—"

"They never found anything," Marilyn said firmly. "And that's the whole story, Chris. The police came and questioned everyone who had been at the seder. They were very nice, very polite. They took notes and asked if there was anything else we wanted to say, any ideas we had on who could have done this, but of course, nobody had any ideas at all. My father was a wreck. My mother almost had a nervous breakdown over it. But they never came up with anything."

"Did they talk to Shirley Finster?"

"They must have. They asked for names of people she worked with and friends and neighbors, and I'm sure we all gave them whatever we knew."

"Do you have a theory of your own?" I asked.

"I never thought of it as a theory. You can imagine I've given a lot of thought to what happened to her. One possibility is that she didn't feel well and instead of worrying us, she grabbed her coat and bag and went downstairs to find a cab and go home. While she was waiting, some stranger grabbed her. If that's what happened, it's as good as saying there's no answer. The other possibility is that she met someone for some reason and he killed her. But I can't tell you why. If that's what happened, she would have gone downstairs to meet whoever it was, give him or tell him whatever she had to give or tell, and planned to come back up before anyone ever noticed she was missing. That's why she had her coat and purse with her. And if I have a theory, that's my theory."

She looked very worn and I said, "Let's take a break."

"Good idea," Mel said. "I'll just boil some water and we'll have tea."

"I can use a cup," her mother said.

5

We talked about other things while we had tea and cake. Marilyn walked over to the window where Mel kept an arrangement of beautiful plants and admired how healthy they looked. I sat and glanced over the notes I had taken. Whatever I had hoped to learn from Marilyn, it wasn't there. As I reviewed what she had said, what popped out at me was the idea that Iris had simply not felt well and decided to go home without making an issue of it. As theories go, it satisfied all the facts I knew, that she had taken her purse and coat, that she had volunteered to open the door for Elijah to excuse herself from the table, that wherever the apartment was located, New York streets are not always the safest place for a single woman to walk at night.

I accepted another cup of tea and removed myself from the mother and daughter, who had begun a conversation that did not involve me. Holding my cup, I sauntered out into the living room. The sun was streaming into the room, highlighting the pieces of colored glass on tables and shelves, bringing out the color in the furniture and rugs. It was a comfortable room, pleasing to the eye and body. The Grosses didn't spend much time

47

here, and it seemed a shame that the prettiest room was used the least.

"There you are." Mel stood at the entrance to the living room. "You slipped away so quietly, I thought you'd gone home."

"Like Aunt Iris," I said.

"Is that what you think, Chris?"

"It's certainly the simplest explanation."

"Come back and join the crowd."

I followed her into the family room, set my cup and saucer down, and sat in my chair. "I really need something to convince me that Iris didn't just decide to go home, maybe because she had a headache, maybe because she was just plain tired."

"She wouldn't have left without saying something," Marilyn said.

"I know that you feel very sure of that, but look at it from my point of view. Here's a sweet, thoughtful woman who's had a big day helping her sister-in-law in the kitchen. She's already drunk a couple of glasses of wine and eaten a big meal. She's exhausted. Maybe tomorrow she's helping someone else prepare another seder, and if she doesn't get home and get a night's sleep, she'll be a wreck. When she gets home, she'll give you a call so you don't worry."

"I see what you mean," Mel said. "You look at it that way—and I'm sure that's the way the police would look at it—and it makes perfect sense. I guess if a neighbor of mine told me that kind of story, I'd be inclined to see it that way myself."

"Does it mean you're giving up?" Marilyn asked.

"It means I have to find something compelling that

someone knows of that's been overlooked that would give me a reason to come up with a different theory."

"How are we going to do that?"

"You said your father still keeps the old apartment."

"Yes. It's a beautiful apartment, prewar, big rooms. It's not in the best condition anymore. It hasn't been painted in years and the curtains are old. After my mother died, it wasn't taken care of as well as before."

"It doesn't matter. May I see it?"

"Of course. I have the key. When would you like to go?" She seemed ready to take me there right away.

"How about tomorrow?"

"Tomorrow's fine." Marilyn smiled. "I thought you were giving up, Chris. You really had me worried."

"I haven't given up, but I need something to explode in front of me, something that screams, 'Look, this woman wasn't just mugged on the way home.' Maybe that apartment will do it. And anyway, I'd like to see it, get a feel for where the seder took place, where the rooms were in relation to each other."

"How's nine-thirty tomorrow morning?"

"Give me the address and I'll be there."

"I don't really know what I'm looking for," I told Jack when he came home from his law school classes. "I just got the feeling while we were talking this afternoon that there was nothing sinister about Iris leaving the seder. She was tired, she saw a chance to slip out with no one watching or asking questions, and she took it, grabbed her pocketbook, put on her coat, opened the door for Elijah, and went home. The tragedy is, she never got there, but I think she may well have been the victim of random violence."

"You're starting to sound like a cop, my lovely wife."

"Is that good or bad?"

"Forget the value judgment. It's what happens when you've investigated a lot of crimes."

"It sounds bad to me," I said. "I thought I had a unique point of view. If I lose it, there goes my advantage."

"You haven't lost your unique point of view, and I don't think you ever will. You just see what the rest of us see, that there are reasonable explanations to crimes, not satisfying explanations, not the kind of answers friends and families want to hear, but answers that fit the facts and often turn out to be the right answers."

"What do you think these people want to hear?" I asked.

"What you said when you first told me about this, what Mel told you, that her aunt was doing something noble, a favor someone asked for, and he killed her. That makes Aunt Iris a hero, a martyr, someone we admire and love even more than before. Nobody wants to know that a beloved relative was killed by a mugger for her jewelry and the couple of bucks in her wallet."

"You're right, that's very painful. There's that sense of a life wasted. It's much harder to accept than a death that resulted from bravery or generosity."

"So there you have it. Who knows? Maybe you'll find some piece of paper in Mel's grandfather's apartment that will explain Iris's death."

"I doubt that. He's alive and has all his faculties. If he knows something, I'm sure he would have told the police or the family."

"Then maybe you'll just have a good time looking around an old apartment. Where was the body found?"

"I forgot to ask. I'll ask Marilyn in the morning. Before I give up on this, I'd like to look at the file."

He gave me his grin. "How'd I guess? We'll get it for you, honey. I just need a precinct. Not to change the subject, but are those Mel's own cookies sitting on the counter?"

"Just waiting for you. You have enough cold chicken to fill all the empty spaces?" I always have something waiting for Jack when he comes home. On a typical day he doesn't have time to eat between his tour at the Sixty-fifth and the start of his first class.

"Plenty. And that was a good tomato. Didn't taste like the plastic one I had for lunch."

"Then dig in. They're all for you."

"Let me at 'em."

The phone rang early in the morning, and I sensed some change in plans was about to happen.

"Chris? It's Marilyn. How are you this morning?"

"I'm fine. Ready to go."

"If you wouldn't mind, I'd like to suggest a little change in our itinerary. I talked to my Aunt Sylvie yesterday. I know you want to talk to her, and I thought I'd try to set something up. She's adamant that you see her before you do anything else. Would you mind?"

"Of course not. When would she like to see me?"

"This morning. Since we were going into the city anyway, I think we can work it out. She lives in the Bronx, on the Grand Concourse. Do you know it?"

"I've heard of it."

"I'll pick you up and we'll drive in together. When

we're finished at Sylvie's, I'll drive us down to Pop's apartment. How's nine o'clock?"

"I'll be ready."

6

Actually, I was a little sorry I wouldn't get to speak to Sylvie alone. I wasn't sure how Marilyn would react to my questioning. Ideally, when you interview someone you want it one on one, without anyone else present who might prompt or contradict the one you're asking. But I decided to set aside my concerns until we reached Aunt Sylvie.

Marilyn picked me up punctually and we drove into the city, talking all the way. When we reached the Grand Concourse, I absolutely gasped.

"It's like the Champs Elysées," I said, looking at the wide center lanes and the narrower side lanes separated by grassy strips. "How does anyone cross from one side to the other?"

"With great care," Marilyn said. "Cars tend to speed and you've got to watch yourself. I'm going to make a U-turn up ahead and see if I can park on Aunt Sylvie's side so we don't have to cross." At the light she swung left, crossing the oncoming lanes, the grassy strip, and finally turning in to the parked-up lane next to the sidewalk.

"There's one," she said.

Sure enough, there was a space just big enough for

one car with a little elbow grease and patience. "Perfect," she said with satisfaction. "It's the next building down. Let's go."

It was a building that had seen better days, but it was reasonably clean and the door to the lobby was locked. Marilyn pushed a button, Aunt Sylvie came on the intercom, then pressed a buzzer that released the lock. A single elevator was heading up when we reached it, the indicator at four. It went to the top floor, the sixth, then made its slow way down to the ground floor. The shaky ride up made me wonder whether the cables were checked periodically, but I kept the thought to myself.

"Here we are," Marilyn said as we stopped with a jolt on five.

Sylvie had the door open and she double-locked it behind us. She was even smaller than I remembered, barely five feet tall and nearly wafer-thin.

"Come in, girls," she said in her high-pitched voice. "Take your coats off and make yourselves comfortable. Hello, Chris. I remember you from the seder."

"It's nice to see you again," I said, realizing that I had no idea what her last name was, having forgotten to check the list of names Mel had given me. "This is a very nice apartment."

"Two bedrooms and two bathrooms. I wouldn't change it for the world, but the neighborhood's not what it used to be. Crime, crime, crime. You can't go out after dark anymore and there's nowhere to shop."

"How do you manage?"

"A few of us get together and take a taxi to the supermarket."

"It's nice you have friends here."

"That's all I have left, a few friends. Sit down. Not

you, Marilyn. I'm not talking to this girl with you around."

"That's fine, Aunt Sylvie. I'll just take the paper and sit in the bedroom."

"There's a TV in the big one in case you finish your paper. Go ahead. We won't miss you."

Marilyn took herself off to the bedroom, and Sylvie and I sat near the window in the living room. It looked out over the Concourse, lined with prewar apartment houses, trees, and people sitting on folding chairs.

"Marilyn told me you're trying to find out who killed my sister."

"I'm giving it a try," I said, reluctant to commit myself at this early stage.

"How much do you know?"

"Just that she left the seder when she opened the door for Elijah, she took her coat and purse with her, and two days later they found her body."

She lifted her hands and dropped them in her lap. "Already you have it wrong. Nobody remembers the way it happened. She didn't go, she was taken. She didn't wear her coat and she didn't take her pocket-book."

"How do you know?"

"Because I know who took her. He was waiting for her. They all know, but they won't tell you."

I started to feel uncomfortable. This was a woman who lived by herself, which meant the family believed she was competent, but she sounded on the edge. "Will you tell me?" I asked.

"She had a friend, a man friend. I knew him. She used to come here with him. He was crazy about her, but he was a very jealous man. He was waiting for her that night at my brother's apartment. When she opened the door, he grabbed her. That's what happened."

"Do you know this man's name?"

"Harry. I don't remember his last name anymore. She went with him for years. He had a lot of money and he was very good looking. They would have gotten married, but he had one of those wives that wouldn't let him go. Iris only wanted him if she could marry him."

"Did you tell the police about him after Iris died?"

"I'm sure I must have. It's a long time ago. I can't remember everything I said."

"Did you remember his name back then?"

"Back then I remembered everything."

"Sylvie, what would Harry have been jealous of?"

"Iris had a new friend."

"She was going out with someone when she died?"

"I think so."

"And Harry knew about it?"

"Of course he knew. If Iris was going out with another man, she couldn't be going out with Harry, could she?"

It sounded pretty logical. "I guess not."

"So he knew and he was jealous. He knew she'd be at my brother's for the seder, and Harry didn't live so far away."

"Did he live in the same building?"

"Not the same building but maybe on the same street. You could ask Abe what Harry's last name is. He knows, but he won't tell you."

"Why do you think he won't tell me?"

"He'll tell you what Iris was doing was her own business. But the truth is, Abe made it his business, too."

"Did Harry ever come to a seder?"

She stopped and thought, her head tilting upwards, her eyes, behind thick glasses, unfocused. "Maybe," she said. "Maybe he came. But not that night. That night Iris came alone."

"Do you remember what happened that night?"

"Like it was yesterday."

"Tell me about it."

"How she disappeared?"

"Everything you remember."

"The whole family was there, Abe and Sarah, *alahe ha shalom*, and their children and grandchildren. Maybe not the youngest. Maybe Sandy wasn't there that night. But Marilyn was there and her brother David and her sister, Naomi, and their children. There were lots of people. I was there because my son was away and my daughter was going to her in-laws that night. So I went to my brother's. Iris was there because Iris never married, so she always went to her brother's seder."

"Excuse me," I interrupted. "You said something after you mentioned Sarah. I didn't quite get it."

"I said in Hebrew, she should rest in peace. She died. Abe's wife died a long time ago."

"I see. Go on. Your memory is very good, Sylvie."

"There's nothing wrong with my memory," she said, contradicting herself. "I have a very good memory. Where was I? So we were all at the table and it came time to open the door for Elijah, and Iris got up and left the room."

"Did she say anything before she left?"

"I don't know. She just got up. Somebody had to open the door. It was easy for her to get up. If I got up, I would have to squeeze myself out, but where Iris was sitting, it was easy. There was no one in the way."

"So she got up and she left the room."

"That's what happened. She got up and she left the room."

I heard a quiver in her voice. The little face looked sad, the hands were clenched into fists. "Do you remember anything else?"

She nodded. "All of a sudden I looked over to where Iris was sitting and she wasn't there. 'Where's Iris?' I said. 'What happened to Iris?' "

"You were the one who noticed she was gone?"

"I was the one. I saw that empty place. Right at that moment I didn't think anything was wrong. I just didn't know where she was. So I called her and she didn't answer. And somebody on that side of the table got up and went to look for her. And we never found her." She took a tissue out of her dress pocket and pushed it under her glasses to touch her eyes. "She was just gone."

"Did you look for her?"

"Everybody looked. I looked, Abe looked, the children looked. This one went to the bedroom, that one went outside, another one called the police."

"You said her coat was still there."

"He grabbed her when she opened the door. Harry. He pulled her out of the apartment and dragged my sister away. She didn't even have time to put her coat on."

"Did the police come?"

"The police came. Two big policemen. They didn't do anything, I can tell you that. This one said she went home, that one said she took a walk. Who takes a walk at eleven o'clock at night in New York? Maybe a policeman does, but my baby sister doesn't. She was this big. She wouldn't walk alone in the middle of the night."

"Did anyone mention Harry to the police?"

"I don't know what anyone said. I was almost having a nervous breakdown. Sarah got me a glass of brandy so I wouldn't pass out. She was a wonderful woman, Sarah. My brother was a lucky man. Are you married?"

"Yes, I am."

"Did I see your husband at the seder?"

"He came late."

"I don't remember him."

She had missed him because her children had taken her from the table when she broke into tears.

"Sylvie, who was the new man Iris was going out with?"

"I couldn't tell you. I never met him."

"Iris never told you his name?"

"If she did, I don't remember."

"Could it have been someone she worked with?"

"I don't think so. The job was a job."

"I heard she worked for a wonderful man, a man who was very generous to her."

"Oh, he was good to her. She wouldn't have worked for him for so long if he hadn't been nice."

"Is it possible he was the new man in her life?"

"Mr. Garganus?" She said it as though it were the most outrageous idea I could have suggested. "Well, I don't think Iris would go out with Mr. Garganus. He was a married man with children. Iris wouldn't go out with someone like that."

"But you said Harry was married, and she went out with him."

"Harry was different. Harry didn't live with his wife anymore."

"Was Iris having any problems around that time?"

"Problems? What kind of problems would she have? She didn't tell me she was having problems. She looked good, she was wearing a nice dress. Iris always looked good. She had a good figure, she took care of herself. It's very important to take care of yourself."

"Sylvie, do you remember Iris's friend Shirley?"

"Shirley Finster? I remember her very well. A lovely person."

"Would you have any idea how I could find her? I think she'd be a good person to talk to."

"Shirley? What could Shirley tell you? She wasn't there that night."

"But she knew Iris well."

"So what? Shirley didn't kill Iris."

"Do you know where Shirley lives now?"

"I don't have any idea. Maybe she moved to Florida." She moved a hand as though to dismiss the subject of Shirley.

"Is there anything else you think I should know, Sylvie? Anything that would help me find her killer?"

"I know one thing," she said, the damp tissue clutched in her hand. "I don't know if I should tell you. Nobody else will."

I waited. "If it would help, then I should know about it," I said.

"I don't know. Abe would kill me if I told."

"Let me give you my phone number, Sylvie. Think about it. You can call me collect and we can talk."

"Oh, that's nice." She smiled. "Yes, let's do that. Let me think about what else I can tell you."

"And if you think of Harry's last name, I'd like that, too."

"Abe will know. Ask him."

"I will." But I had no desire to ask her brother. I felt he had enough troubles of his own right now that raking up this terrible event would not be in his best interests.

"Then we're finished," Sylvie said with satisfaction, as though she had just been excused from the dentist's chair. "I'll get Marilyn."

I stood by the window, hearing their voices from the bedroom. Downstairs cars sped by, young mothers looking carefully before pushing their strollers across the Concourse. I had never seen the Champs Elysées, but if it was as beautiful as this wide thoroughfare, it must be truly magnificent.

We said our good-byes quickly, Sylvie obviously finished with us and not anxious to have us dawdle. The sound of the bolt being turned echoed down the hall as we walked to the elevator.

7

Marilyn was smiling. "My aunt is a character, isn't she?"

"Quite a character. You said she was so anxious to talk to me, but it seemed as though she was much more anxious to get rid of us."

"Did you learn anything useful?"

"I'm not sure. She said Iris had a man friend named Harry who she went out with for years."

"Oh my goodness, Harry. I forgot all about Harry. What did she tell you?"

"Not much, just that he was married and couldn't get a divorce, which was why they never married, and I gather they never lived together. She said Iris didn't want that kind of relationship. Did you know him, Marilyn?"

"I certainly met him, but it was a long time ago. He was a tall, good-looking man, dark hair, nice smile. He adored her, I can tell you that."

"Do you remember his last name?"

We were in the street now, walking to the car. "If I ever knew it, it's gone now. I bet it's thirty years since I first met him."

"Do you know what he did?"

"No idea." She unlocked the car. "He was just Aunt Iris's guy. I think she brought him around once when Melanie was a baby and he was very sweet to her, cooed at her. A nice man."

We started down the Concourse, staying on the service road. At a light we turned right into a busy street with shops and people and cars, an elevated subway just down the hill. "It's like a little city," I said.

"Anywhere else it would be a city. Here it's a neighborhood. We're heading west now. Pretty soon we'll be at the northern end of Manhattan. Then we'll go downtown to my father's apartment."

"Marilyn, is there any family gossip about Iris that you can remember?"

"Like what?"

"Having to do with Harry or another boyfriend, some relationship that might have caused the family a problem?"

"There may have been. I may have heard some whispers, but I can't tell you anything more than that. Remember I was the next generation, and if my parents, my aunts and uncles, knew something they weren't happy about, they would try to keep it to themselves."

"Sylvie said Iris's boss was Mr. Garganus."

"That's it!" Marilyn said excitedly. "Wilfred Garganus. I recognized it the minute you said it. Sylvie's memory's not that bad, is it?"

"It's pretty good, actually. But she may be holding something back." I didn't want to say more. I felt in an awkward situation. If there was something embarrassing about Iris's life, I didn't want it to get out to the family without the permission of the generation that was keeping it secret. "Have you given any thought to whether

Iris could have been having an affair with Mr. Garganus?"

"I really don't think so," Marilyn said as though she had just now considered it. "I think she was very fond of him, but I don't think it went any further than that."

"You know, Iris could have been having an affair with Mr. Garganus, or with someone else, after a long relationship with Harry ended, and she still might have been killed by a mugger when she slipped out of the seder to go home."

"That's true. And you may dig up some unpleasant things about Iris that we'd all rather had never been unearthed and still not find out who killed her or why. Her life may have nothing to do with her death."

"Exactly."

"So what are you telling me?"

"I want a reason to continue, some piece of information that was overlooked, some motive, something I can sink my teeth into."

"Well, we'll be at Pop's soon. Maybe it'll turn up."

I could see why Abraham Grodnik wanted to hang on to his apartment. The building was like many others, a pale beige brick with a façade flush with the sidewalk, a design that made the most of the available space, leaving nothing for a plant or a tree. But the location was irresistible, East Seventy-first Street, just a brisk walk from the beautiful shops on Madison and Lexington Avenues. And the apartment, when we got up there, had large rooms, including a sunken living room, a kitchen large enough for a family to eat in, and two bathrooms.

"It's wonderful," I said.

"A nice place to grow up. My parents were the first family to live in this apartment. My mother used to tell us how she came down the day they began renting and got in line. The ones on higher floors were two or three dollars a month more, so she always thought she got a real bargain on the fourth floor."

"Two or three dollars a month," I said with amazement.

"It's hard to believe anyone could think of that as a big saving, but remember, we're talking about a time when stamps were three cents, a letter from one part of New York to another was only two, and penny postcards were guess how much. The rent on this apartment was under a hundred dollars."

I shook my head. "It sounds like the way I used to think of money when I was at the convent. You spent only what you needed to, and if you could save a nickel or a dime, you were ahead of the game—or you bought yourself an ice cream cone."

"It's not a bad way to grow up," Marilyn said. "Sometimes I wish I'd been able to instill a little of my mother's thriftiness in my children. Anyway, here we are. It's probably a little dusty—we don't have it cleaned every week anymore—but you're welcome to look around, open drawers, whatever you'd like."

"I don't know what good opening drawers would be. Iris didn't live here." I looked around at the furniture and the pictures on the walls. "Your mother must have been a great collector. Everything looks very special."

"She loved antiques. She loved china. Sometimes I'd walk into a room and catch her standing and looking at a shelf of her treasures with a smile on her face. It gave her pleasure just to look at them."

"I can see why." We were next to a cabinet that contained a collection of dishes, each one different, each beautiful. "Show me where the seder was that night."

We walked into the dining room, turning a corner that obscured the front door. The furniture was mahogany, dark and heavy and very traditional.

"We had to open up the table to get everyone seated. Iris was somewhere over here, close to the doorway. Pop was at the head of the table, over at that end." She pointed to the farthest place from the doorway. "You can see that wherever you sat, you couldn't see the front door without getting up and actually leaving the room."

"Where was your mother sitting?"

"Opposite my father, down at this end. This is closest to the kitchen."

"And not far from where Iris sat."

"That's right."

I took my notebook and made a very rough sketch of the apartment. Then, on another page, I drew in the dining room in more detail. "You said the children sat separately. Where were they?"

"They were in the kitchen that night. And they couldn't see the front door any more than we could."

"I think you told me the women left their pocketbooks on a table somewhere."

"Out here."

I followed her into the foyer, where a chair, a table, and a mirror were the only furniture.

"They left things on the floor, on the table, on the chair. I'm sure some people must have come with shopping bags, and those might have ended up out here, too."

"This must be the coat closet you mentioned," I said, opening a door near the door to the apartment.

"That's it. It's very deep, and Mom used to joke that it was the attic for the apartment. In the winter the winter coats were on the front rack and the summer things on the back one. There's also room for suitcases back there, and I think that's where Mom kept them."

"Did the guests hang their coats in this closet at the seder or were they put on a bed in one of the bedrooms?"

"Probably both. If you came early, there was room in the closet. Later on you probably had to toss your coat on a bed. But Aunt Iris came early that day, I'm sure of that, so she would have hung her coat in the closet. And you know, if she'd put it on a bed, Mom would have found it the next day."

"Right. Marilyn, why don't we just look at what's hanging here? The question of whether Iris was wearing her coat is still a little unclear."

"That's what we're here for." She leaned inside and item by item, she pulled the hangers across the bar and we looked at each one. "Pop's raincoat, his old winter coat I told him to throw out years ago, his old raincoat that's falling apart. I wish he'd put a light in this closet like we told him to when we were kids, but he wouldn't listen to us. What's this?"

It was a woman's coat, a soft chocolate brown. Marilyn took it off the hanger. "It's Mom's," she said sadly. "Hanging there all these years. I guess Pop didn't want to give it away. Isn't it beautiful? She got it a few months before she died."

I touched the fabric. It was as soft as cashmere. "It is beautiful. But you're sure it was your mother's?"

"Absolutely." She dug in the pockets and pulled out a pair of leather gloves and a couple of tissues. "It's Mom's. This is too big to be Iris's anyway. Iris probably wore a size eight."

There were several empty hangers and little else on the front rack. I assumed that Abraham had taken his warm clothes with him when he moved into his daughter's apartment.

"What's in the back?" I asked.

"Let's take a look." Marilyn pushed aside the winter clothes so that we could walk to the back of the large closet. Then we went through the summer things. "There isn't much anymore," she said. "I remember when this closet was so packed you couldn't get your hand between two hangers, but with everyone gone except Pop, there isn't much here. That was Mom's suitcase over there." She bent and pulled it forward. "They used to enjoy traveling when they were younger. Pop's is probably with him. Anything else you want to see?"

I backed out of the closet. "I really just wanted to see if Iris's coat could have gone unnoticed. It doesn't seem to be there."

"We would have found it, I'm sure. My goodness, look at all these boots. You'd think we lived in Siberia. These must have been my mother's. I'll have to give them away." She lifted a pair of shoe boots and set them aside. "For heaven's sake, look at this." She pulled something out into the better light of the foyer.

"What is it?"

"Mom's old black pocketbook." She opened it. "There's still money in the wallet. Pop probably couldn't bear to go through it, so he just left it there." She rummaged around. "Here's the silver pen I got her from Tiffany's for her birthday. I always wondered if she used it." She held it in her hand for a moment, then replaced it in the bag. "Her cents-off coupons for the grocery. The little leather book she marked down her appointments in. Here's the dentist in January. I wish Pop had gotten rid of this."

"I'm sorry to do this to you, Marilyn."

"It's not your fault." She closed the bag and put it down on the floor of the closet. "Well, let's see what else is lurking here among the boots." She moved things. "Not much. Let's have a look at the other side."

I couldn't see what she was doing because her body was in the way. I stood back, wondering if this had been such a good idea. There was nothing here that could help me. The layout of the apartment convinced me Iris had been totally unseen the moment she left the dining room.

"Here's another bag," Marilyn said, standing up. She brushed her dress off. "It's awfully dusty in there. I'll have to make sure the closet gets vacuumed next time we have someone in. I don't remember this one. Maybe it's my sister's." She opened it and looked inside. "Isn't that a beauty?" she said. "Leather lined. You don't see that much anymore." She pulled something out, a leather case that held credit cards. "That's funny."

"What is it?"

"Mom's credit cards were in the other bag." She pulled one card out of its slot and her face changed. "Oh, Chris."

"What is it, Marilyn?"

"It's Iris's American Express card. This isn't Mom's bag, it's Iris's. It's the bag she carried the night of the seder." She turned to look at me, the dusty bag in her hand. "This has been sitting on the floor of the closet for sixteen years."

8

We sat in the living room, more or less recovering from the shock. The handbag was indeed Iris Grodnik's. Her French purse, full of money, was inside, along with her credit cards, a pen and pencil, a lipstick, an elegant mirror, and a compact with face powder.

"She must have put it in the closet when she came, just pushed it over to the side where it would be out of the way," Marilyn said. "No one would have noticed it if they weren't actually looking for it, and I certainly thought all the purses were in the foyer."

"It means she intended to come back," I said. "She didn't just decide to go home, she didn't go out to buy anything because her money is here, and she wasn't grabbed when she opened the door as Sylvie thinks she was because she had her coat on."

"She went to meet someone," Marilyn said.

"Or out for a breath of fresh air."

"Don't believe it. She wouldn't have done that. This is what you've been looking for, Chris. This is proof that Iris was killed by someone she met, and she must have met him outside the building or she would have left her coat behind."

"Marilyn, Sylvie said the man that Iris went with for

many years, Harry, lived not far from this apartment. I
think we have to find out what his last name is and
cross our fingers that he's still alive so we can talk to
him."

"Sylvie said that? That Harry lived near Pop and
Mom?"

"That's what she told me."

"I'm not sure I ever knew where he lived. Whenever
I saw him it was with Iris, and that would have been
here or at Iris's apartment. Why can't I think what his
last name was?"

I took out my notebook. "I need to fill in some geog-
raphy. Where did Iris live at the time of her death?"

"Kips Bay. She had a beautiful apartment."

"I've heard of that, but I don't really know where it
is."

"On the east side in the Thirties, just south of the
UN."

"So she was on the East Side, too."

"Yes. And one of the reasons she picked that location
was that it was easy to get up to Pop's. She liked to
keep close to the family."

"I'd like to look at the place she lived if we have
time today. Not that I can learn anything, but it gives
me a feel for Iris's life."

"We can drive there after lunch. Anything else?"

"You've never told me where Iris's body was found."

"Yes, of course." Marilyn stopped as though the
thought of the location was a painful memory. "It was
a terrible place, Chris. Up at the northern tip of Manhattan there are oil yards. They're about a block from
Broadway and quite near Baker Field, the stadium
where Columbia plays its football games. It's a place

where oil comes in on big barges and is stored until it's taken away by truck to be delivered. I never knew this place even existed, but that's where they found poor Iris's body two days after she disappeared."

"How awful," I said. I jotted down as much as I could of what Marilyn had just described. "That means that whoever killed her must have had a car."

"I certainly think so. My husband and I drove up there about a week after they found Iris, just to see what kind of a place it was. There's a chain-link fence around it—with enough holes that you could probably push a body through if you tried, or squeeze inside yourself if you were crazy enough to want to do it. The fence was all overgrown with weeds, and there's litter around. It's an awful place." She stopped for a moment.

"What's inside the fence?"

"Mostly oil tanks, a little shack where a guard probably dozes all night, the cabs of old oil trucks. I suppose you want to see it." She sounded unhappy at the prospect.

"Not if it's too painful for you."

"Death is painful. Iris's death was very painful. Who would take her to such a place, Chris?"

"Someone who didn't want her found, someone vicious enough to kill her, someone, I'm sure, with a car."

"Yes, he must have had a car. He couldn't very well have taken her there by cab."

I glanced at my watch. "You must be starving. It's a long time since we left Oakwood."

"Let's have lunch. There are plenty of places around, and it's my treat."

"Thank you."

"Let me get a bag first. You'll take Iris's purse home

with you and give it a good once-over. Maybe you'll learn something the police didn't know."

"I'll do my best."

"That's all we ask."

Marilyn always seems to know some wonderful place to eat, wherever she happens to be. Today was no exception. We walked into a little restaurant on Lexington Avenue that managed to have exactly one small table for two empty, and we sat down to a lovely lunch.

"I think I'll have the salade niçoise," Marilyn said, her face half-covered with the menu.

"A what?" I asked.

"Niçoise," she explained. "That means it's from Nice, you know, the city in the south of France."

"Yes, of course," I said with some embarrassment, remembering high school French a few minutes too late. "What's in it?"

"Lots of nice things, tuna, potatoes, green beans, little cherry tomatoes, even some anchovies."

It was the tuna that caught my attention. "I'll give it a try. It sounds good, and I don't think I've ever had it."

"You and Jack should think about a vacation in Europe sometime. He gets a lot of vacation time, doesn't he?"

"He does, but he's always working on his law books."

"How's he doing?"

"Not bad," I said with pride. "He was very unsure of himself when he began, but he's gained a lot of self-confidence. I think he was afraid he'd be looked down on because he's over thirty and a cop. But he's gotten some admiration for both of those things. He has first-hand knowledge that almost no one else has, and there have been a couple of times when he was able to quote a relevant part of a law."

"I'm glad he's as smart as he is nice. I could tell the minute I met him he was a good man. He looks you in the eye when he talks to you, and I think that's very important."

It was more a comment on Marilyn, I thought, than on Jack, but I thanked her for her kind words. Marilyn is a very aboveboard person. That's probably why she gets along so well with her adult daughter. She doesn't manipulate. If there's something going on in Mel's life that she doesn't approve of or has questions about, she asks openly. I suppose childless people always have strong feelings about how to raise children—and they're often wrong—but I liked the way Marilyn and her daughter interacted, and I always sensed the respect each had for the other, over and above the affection.

My salad was a happy new culinary experience, although Marilyn assured me they were better in Nice. For my part I was delighted they were this good on Lexington Avenue.

"When we finish, I'll pick up the car and we'll drive down to Kips Bay. Then what?" Marilyn asked.

"Well, it's been a long day. Jack and I can take a ride over the weekend. He can tell me what precinct it's in, and I'll see if I can find the detective who handled the case."

"Do you think he's still there? Sixteen years is a long time."

"If he isn't, he's probably somewhere else in the city. And in any case, Jack can get a copy of the file and go through it with me."

"It doesn't sound like fun. It must be a very nasty job, reading autopsy reports and looking at ugly pictures of victims."

"It is. But you keep telling yourself, this is going to help me find a killer."

"A beautiful little woman that didn't weigh a hundred pounds. I will never be able to accept what happened to her."

"How did she die, Marilyn?" I asked. It was a question I needed an answer to, but she had never volunteered it and I had been reluctant to ask.

"She was beaten to death," Marilyn said sadly. "I think he broke her neck."

"How awful," I said aloud, and to myself I thought: This was no case of random violence. He hated her.

We picked up Marilyn's car after we finished our coffee and drove down Second Avenue from the Seventies to the Thirties. A couple of turns and we were in front of a magnificent apartment house overlooking the East River.

"It's beautiful," I said. "Iris lived well."

"They paid her well and she was single. Single women can afford a lot of things married couples can't. Nice apartments are one of them."

"Mel said she and her cousins inherited Iris's money."

"That's right. Iris had a will. She was a very modern woman for her age. She divided her money equally among her grandnieces and -nephews. But there wasn't much. We're talking about hundreds, not thousands or tens of thousands."

"What about her other things? She must have owned jewelry."

"She did, and a nice fur coat. I think Harry gave her most of it. I asked Pop about it over the weekend. Those things were to be distributed to her remaining brothers and sisters. I think Sylvie got the coat."

"So nothing went to your generation."

"We didn't need it. Sixteen years ago we were all in the prime of life. Are you looking for a motive in the family?"

"I'm looking for a motive wherever I can find one. What about boyfriends? Did any of them inherit?"

"Not that I remember."

"Do you have a copy of her will?"

"I don't think so. I didn't inherit, so none was sent to me. But Mel should have gotten one. She was an heir."

"Yes, she mentioned that."

"Have you seen enough?"

"I think so."

"Then let's call it a day."

9

Marilyn dropped me off at my house and drove down the block to look in on Mel and the grandchildren. The first thing I did was change into a pair of jeans, a shirt, and a warm sweater. The heat would take a while and the house was cold. One thing I learned well as a Franciscan nun was how to pinch pennies. While I had absolute financial security at St. Stephen's, I rarely had a nickel more than I needed on any given day. I don't leave the house with fifty cents in my bag anymore, but I keep track of what I have, and sometimes I have a little trouble letting go of it, even when I should.

As soon as I changed my clothes, I sat down at the dining room table and emptied Iris's bag piece by piece. The purse itself, as Marilyn had noted, was well made of a beautiful black leather with a striking red leather lining and a small change purse of the same red leather anchored to a seam with a fine gold chain. The change purse held her subway tokens and what looked like a mailbox key. The French purse, which was also bright red leather, had seventy-two dollars in it plus some change. It also held her Social Security card, a library card, and some membership cards to organizations I was not familiar with.

The credit card case was separate and contained quite a number of cards. There was the American Express card Marilyn had pulled out when she first opened the case, cards for Bloomingdale's, Saks, Lord & Taylor, Bergdorf Goodman, and B. Altman. My Aunt Meg used to love shopping at Altman's, but it had closed down some time ago, long after Iris's death. There was also a Visa card and one gasoline card, although I had not found a driver's license anywhere.

The bag was divided into two sections, the rear one holding the French purse and credit cards, the front containing keys, tissues, a lipstick, the mirror, and a small red leather book. This last was an agenda with the week on two pages, a red ribbon marking the place where "seder" was noted on two consecutive days, and under the second was the letter *M*. I sat back, turned to January, and began looking at every entry Iris had made.

Iris Grodnik had lived an active life. In her last three months she had attended the theater several times, an opera at Lincoln Center, a lecture at Cooper Union, a wedding in February, two birthday parties, a few family affairs, and a funeral about a week before she died. Some of the entries were so cryptic I could not determine what they meant. "*L*'s wedding 4" on a Sunday referred, I assumed, to the person and the time of the event. Whether Dr. J. was a doctor or a dentist—or perhaps a chiropractor—I could not tell. Appointments continued beyond the date of her death. Had she lived, she would have attended a bridal shower for *C* on a Saturday afternoon. I took a sheet of paper and wrote down the family events, including the shower, to ask Marilyn about. I didn't know if that would lead anywhere, but I had little else to work on. I also made a list of all the letters Iris used, presumably to refer to people, the *M* of the second seder, Dr. J., the *C* of the shower, and several others throughout the little book.

What struck me was the absence of any reference to her friend Shirley Finster, or to Harry, the presumed boyfriend. Perhaps she hadn't bothered noting with whom she attended the plays and operas since she would remember that without a reminder. And what about all those empty pages on Saturday nights, the traditional going-out night for single people? Did she have a steady beau for those evenings?

I looked at my watch and decided it was time to think about dinner. I had some lamb and vegetables to stew, and the preparation would take a while. This being Friday, Jack would be home for dinner barring a problem at work.

I browned the meat and cleaned the vegetables, appreciating the aroma from the pot. The house had warmed nicely, and cooking helped to make the kitchen even warmer and more inviting. When everything had been added, the pot covered and the flame turned down to a simmer, I boiled some water in my Christmas present from St. Stephen's, a whistling teakettle, and got some tea out of the cabinet. Then I sat at the kitchen table with the paper and my cup of tea to enjoy the pleasure of my own company.

When the phone rang a little before six, the time when Jack would ordinarily be leaving the station house, I sensed that my evening would be disrupted.

"Hi, honey," Jack's voice said. "How'd it go?"

"More interesting than either of us thought. We found something in Marilyn's closet. I have a lot of things to talk to you about."

"It'll have to wait, Chris. There's a problem."

"You on a case?"

"No. It's family."

I felt a disquieting chill. His father had seen a doctor recently, and his mother had seemed worried about it. "Your dad?"

"No. He's fine. It's something else. I can't talk about it now. Look, I know it's lousy, but I'm going to spend the night at Mom's. I'll be back tomorrow afternoon."

"Jack, is someone sick?"

"Nobody's sick. There's just something I've got to work out here. You don't mind staying alone, do you?"

"I'll be fine."

"Make a reservation for dinner tomorrow, OK?"

"OK."

"I'm really sorry, honey."

"I just hope everything's all right."

"We'll work it out. I'll see you tomorrow."

I sat down at the kitchen table feeling empty and bereft. Although I had spent some nights away from him over the Christmas holiday, Jack had never spent a night away from me. He had sounded strange over the phone, and his explanation had been vague. If it wasn't illness, what else could it be? His parents were reasonably young and reasonably healthy. They both worked and had begun taking trips in the last few years for their vacations. I thought about calling them but decided not to interfere. For the first time since my marriage, I felt excluded from Jack's family, and Jack's family is pretty much the only family I have.

It didn't help that my fragrant stew was on the stove and that I had a million things I wanted to talk to Jack about. I sat for a few minutes, recovering as though I had had the wind knocked out of me. Then I went back to the phone and called Greenwillow, where Gene lived, and arranged for him to visit me for dinner.

"You called just in time," the aide who answered the phone said. "We're almost ready to sit down."

"I'll be there in five minutes. Don't let him eat a bite."

"You got it," she said with a laugh.

I put my coat on and went out to the car.

We had a good time together, my cousin and I. We grew up together in the happy years when both my parents were alive and both of his were, too. During the years when I was a nun, I drove to Oakwood regularly to visit him. He was the reason I owned a car, the reason Aunt Meg maintained a room for me in this very house, covering the bathroom mirror before my arrival and uncovering it after I left. They were all that was left of my family, and now it was only Gene.

We ate together and then, because I knew he would appreciate it, I took him out for ice cream before dropping him off at Greenwillow. Then I went home, read for a while, and went to bed.

It wasn't the best night of my life. I read for a long time, till the words were swimming and I could no longer keep my mind on what I was reading. I turned off the light and fell asleep quickly, but I awoke about an hour later and worried about what it was that had kept my husband away from me. I had no answers, no hints, no vague ideas. Eventually I slept.

The phone rang when the night was still dark and I was disoriented and groggy. I reached for Jack and had a shock when I felt his absence, then found the phone and answered.

"It's me. I'm sorry to get you up."

"Jack?"

"Yes. You OK?"

"I think so. I was sleeping." The way I felt, I still was.

"I can't talk long. I'm in the kitchen and I don't want to wake everybody up."

"Did something happen?"

"I just missed you."

"Oh, that's nice. I miss you, too."

"I'll see you later."

"OK."

"Go back to sleep."

"Mm." It was a piece of advice I didn't need.

His car turned in to the driveway just before three and I went to the door to meet him. We hugged as though we hadn't seen each other in months and then we kissed like lovers meeting at a trysting place.

"We going somewhere for dinner?" he said, taking off his coat.

"I called Ivy's and they said they had a table at seven." Ivy's was a small French restaurant in the next town where you could bring your own wine and the food was good and not very expensive.

"Good. I'm in the mood for Ivy's."

"Do I get to hear what the problem is or do I start biting my fingernails?"

"Anything but that. Can I make some coffee? Mom's started drinking decaf and I need a shot of high octane."

"Go to it."

He was already in the kitchen. "It's my sister," he said.

"Your *sister*."

"She and her friend Taffy have been building up their catering business, doing better and better, everything looking real good, and suddenly—" He stopped and got the coffeemaker going.

"Suddenly what?"

"Suddenly the impossible happens. You hear about these things, but you never think it'll happen to you. Taffy took a vacation. She'd been planning this for months, got tickets to somewhere, hotels, everything. She leaves last weekend, and yesterday morning Eileen gets a call from her bank that the catering account is overdrawn."

"A check bounced?"

"She wrote a check a couple of days ago, and today she's told there isn't enough in the account to cover it. But she knows for sure there's plenty of money there."

I could feel ice work its way down my neck. "Her partner?"

"Taffy emptied out the checking account before she took off."

"That's terrible."

"It's worse than terrible. It's grand larceny."

"You think she stole the money, Jack?"

"She wrote the check and cashed it at the bank before she left. It's her signature; the girl at the bank remembers cashing it for her."

"I can't believe it."

"Eileen can't either. They've been friends since first grade at St. Margaret's."

"Friends don't do things like that," I said.

"Chris, honey, friends do everything enemies do."

"She must be a wreck."

"She is. She's scheduled to do a big party next week-end, they've put down a hefty deposit, and she doesn't have enough money to pay the bills for it. She's a very together person and I've never seen her like this. But what's really eating her is that Taffy would do this. Those girls grew up together. Taffy was always under-foot. I used to step on her when she was a kid."

"Something must've happened to make her do this."

"It wasn't spur of the moment, Chris. She didn't wake up one morning and turn crazy and decide to empty the checking account and hop on a bus. She planned this for weeks, maybe for months."

"Eileen's heart must be broken."

"It is. Broken into little pieces. But the important thing right now is to keep the business going. If Eileen disappoints this client next week, they could take her to court and that could be the end of her."

"How much is involved?"

"She wasn't clear on that. She just isn't thinking straight at this point. But I think Dad and I can come up with a couple of thousand to get her through. She has almost nothing of her own in savings because she wanted to keep a comfortable cushion in the business account."

"Jack, I have whatever she needs."

"Forget it. That's your money. You know what Ar-nold Gold would say if I let you use that money for Eileen's business?"

Arnold Gold is the lawyer I met on my first case, the man I work for, the substitute father who gave me away at our wedding last August. He is also a person very

concerned about protecting me from dangers I can neither see nor imagine.

"Jack, this isn't a question of you letting me do anything with the money. You just said it's my money. Last
I looked, I was an adult of reasonable intelligence and
a mind of my own. I happen to have plenty of cash in
that account because one of the bonds Aunt Meg bought
just came due. Let me think of this as an investment. Investments don't always yield cash dividends. Sometimes they help deserving people."

"Chris, I can't let you—" He stopped to rephrase. "I
don't think it's a good idea. That's your inheritance. It's
there for you, your future, your old age. Look, the truth
is, you may never get it back. I don't know if Eileen
can handle this business by herself, and she's in no
shape right now to go looking for a new partner, not
that she could trust anyone ever again after this."

"Then let me give it to her as a gift."

"Did anyone ever tell you you were impossible to
reason with?"

"Dozens of people, most of them students who
thought I was cruel, heartless, and totally devoid of
understanding."

He shook his head. "We'll talk about it tomorrow."

He meant that. He refused for the rest of the day to
discuss his sister's problems. I suggested I could call
her, and he said he thought it wasn't such a good idea.
Eileen and her mother were working together to prepare
for the party next weekend, and Eileen was too close to
tears to carry on a conversation. Exhausted from his
long ordeal last night, Jack took a nap, waking with just
enough time to shower and dress for dinner at Ivy's.

On the way, we stopped at a liquor store and he picked up a bottle of red wine. "OK," he said, getting back in the car. "Now tell me about the mysterious disappearance and death of Aunt Iris."

"I found something that was overlooked for sixteen years."

"Hell, I could've told you you would. You take this stuff seriously. What did you find?"

"Her pocketbook, the one she had with her that night and everyone thought she took with her because they didn't find it in the apartment."

"So you turned the light on and there it was."

I laughed. "It was a little like that, now that I think of it."

"Sitting in the open for sixteen years and no one ever saw it?"

"It was on the floor of a big coat closet, off to the left, with a bunch of boots and umbrellas in front of it. If anyone ever saw it, they probably thought it belonged to Marilyn's mother. But the truth is, I don't think anyone ever saw it. It was in a corner. It was black. Iris had probably pushed it there so it would be out of the way. That family lived in that apartment for fifty years or more. If they cleaned out the closet, it was probably to take down a coat or jacket to give it away. When's the last time you bought a new pair of rubbers or boots?"

"Don't embarrass me. Well, this is really great news. You found evidence pointing to the fact that she didn't pick up and decide to go home, and you've got all sorts of goodies inside that may give you some leads."

"Right on both. Her wallet's in there, her credit cards, a little engagement book with lots of things noted, that kind of stuff. And I can tell you where the body was found."

"OK."

"In the oil yards at the top of Manhattan."

"Way up there?"

"Marilyn said it's near Baker Field."

"Nice part of town," he said caustically. "But the view is good. You can see the East Bronx, the West Bronx, and New Jersey. What else is there in life?" He pulled into a space in front of Ivy's, grabbed the bottle of wine, and we went in. As usual, it was packed, but our table was ready and we were seated right away. Jack ordered Stoly, and I passed. The wine would be enough for me.

"That oil yard is in the Three-Four," he said, as though our conversation had not been interrupted. "I know someone there, I just have to think who."

"That's great, Jack. I'd really hate to walk in cold off the street and start asking questions."

"Won't happen, I promise. I'll find—oh, I know who it is, Greg Jarvis. We took a course together a couple of years ago and then got together on a funny case. He's a nice guy. I'll give him a call."

"How likely is it he was there sixteen years ago?"

"Not very. He's about my age, maybe a year or two older. Sixteen years ago we were just kids. But we'll find the guy who was on the case. And if we can't, there's always the file. Anyway, you can be pretty sure she didn't get up there herself if she left her money in the apartment."

"Also her subway tokens. They're in a separate change purse. I don't believe she would have taken a token and nothing else and then got lost in the subway."

"Doesn't make sense. Either she went downstairs to meet someone or she went out for a walk. Either way, it sounds like a deliberate murder, probably someone with a car."

"That's what I think."

"Not that the detective in charge is going to do much about it at this late date, but what you've got is evidence in a homicide, so you'll have to turn it in."

"I will. Now tell me about Kips Bay. Who was Mr. Kips?"

"Mr. Kip. Jacob, a Dutch farmer. He owned the property around what was called the 'bay.' It's all been filled in now and it's loaded with high-rise buildings, and that whole area in the East Thirties is called Murray Hill."

"Just a little piece of New York history you picked up along the way."

"Why not? It's my city. There was a major confrontation there between gangs and police in the 1863 draft riots."

"You really do know everything," I said with wonder.

"Read the menu. I'm starved."

10

Sunday we relaxed. Jack made breakfast and we picked up Gene on the way to mass. In the afternoon, while Jack read for his Monday night law classes, I scoured Iris Grodnik's pocketbook, making notes of everything she had, a list of all her credit cards, even the brand and color of the lipstick she wore. Since I had to give up this very valuable piece of evidence, I wanted to be certain I would be able to recall every item it contained. Only then did I reluctantly agree with myself that I would turn it over to the police.

When I had completed my notes, I called Marilyn.

"Chris, how nice to hear from you," she said warmly. "How are things going?"

"Jack has a friend at the precinct where the oil yards are located, and I'm going to try to get down there tomorrow. But right now I have a couple of questions to ask you."

"OK."

"In Iris's little engagement book, she's written an *M* on the day of the second seder. She never seems to write names to go with her appointments. Can you think what the *M* for that day might mean?"

"Well, my name is an *M* and so is Mel's. Maybe she meant she would see one or both of us."

"Do you recall where the second seder was going to be?"

"It would have been different for everyone, but maybe Iris was going to Queens to my brother's."

"Your brother Dave?"

"Yes. He lived in Queens at the time."

"Question number two. She has a bridal shower noted for the Saturday after Passover. The initial there is *C*. Whose shower do you suppose that was?"

"A shower for a *C*? Offhand, I can't think who that would be. When was Carol married?" she asked herself. Then she said, "Chris, that's impossible."

"Why?"

"Because Jews can't get married between Passover and Shavuoth."

"I don't understand."

"There are no Jewish weddings during that period. No rabbi will perform a wedding ceremony. If you don't get married before Passover, you just have to wait. I can't imagine a bridal shower two months before a wedding. It seems a little early."

"I wonder whose shower it could be then."

"Maybe someone's at work. Iris was very close to the girls at work."

"So you're pretty sure it wasn't a family affair?"

"Positive."

"Then I guess that's it. I'll keep you posted."

Jack and I had a brief conversation about his sister's problems and my proposed solution, but the upshot was, let's wait a day or so and see. I agreed to wait.

On Monday morning Jack called a little while after he got to the Six-Five, the precinct where he works in Brooklyn and where I had met him while investigating my first case. "Got hold of Greg a little while ago," he said. "He's still at the Three-Four."

"That's great."

"What's even greater, he checked the Grodnik file, and the original detective on the case is also there."

"Terrific."

"His name's Harris White, and Greg says he'll see you whenever you want."

"Can I call him?"

"Sure." He gave me the number. "Greg's told him you're my wife, so you can expect the royal treatment."

"Do I have to wear my diamond tiara?"

"Ah, hold that for another visit. You going today?"

"Can you think of a better time?"

"No, ma'am. Enjoy."

I promised I would and called the Thirty-fourth Precinct and talked to Detective Harris White. He'd been expecting my call and was, he said, looking forward to my visit. I told him I would be there in an hour and a half, and he said that would be fine. I put Iris's purse back in the shopping bag and was on my way.

Having left time for losing my way, I got to the station house on Broadway near 182nd Street early. The desk sergeant pointed me to the stairs, and I went up to the squad room. As I entered the door marked 34th Detective Squad, I noticed a wooden replica of a gold and blue detective shield on the wall with slots for name boards. Two of the slots were filled. Det. White and Det. Farbman were "in."

"Help you?" the man at the nearest desk said as I entered.

"I'm looking for Detective Harris White."

"Over there by the window, ma'am."

"Thank you." The man at the desk by the window had his back to me. I walked over and he turned as I got there. He was in his early forties or thereabouts, black, closer to trim than most of the detectives I had met, and had a nice smile, which he used to greet me.

"Mrs. Brooks, glad to meet you." He offered a hand and shook mine firmly. "I'm Detective Harris White. Please sit down. I hear you're interested in one of my first cases."

"Iris Grodnik. I'm a friend of the family."

"Well, I can tell you, that's one case I would like to lay to rest. I caught it about a week after I got my gold shield, and I was young and cocky and figured I'd close it pretty quick. Now it's sixteen years later and I don't know any more than I knew a couple of days after they found the body."

I put the shopping bag on his desk. "I found something, Detective."

"Harris. We're friends, OK?"

"Fine. I'm Chris."

He looked inside the bag, murmured something I couldn't hear, and pulled out the black leather purse. "Her handbag?"

"Yes."

"Where in God's name did you find this?"

"In the closet in the apartment she was visiting the night she disappeared."

"They told us her purse and coat were gone."

"They were wrong. Her coat was gone, but this was

pushed into a corner and probably hasn't been moved or seen since that night."

"That must be one hell of a closet."

He had it open and was looking at the contents as I had over the weekend. "Money, keys, credit cards, a little date book. Looks like she left everything in it when she walked out of that apartment."

"It does to me, too."

"So she definitely planned to go back for it before she went home."

"Without those keys she couldn't have gotten into her own apartment."

"I'll be damned."

"Was she wearing her coat when she was found?" I asked.

"Oh yeah, she had her coat on, had a nice dress on, no evidence of sexual assault. Whatever he wanted from her, it wasn't sex and it sure wasn't what's in this bag."

"So it could have been something she told him or it could have been something she was carrying with her."

"That's about it."

"Can you tell me how she died?"

"Before we get into that, can you tell me exactly what your interest in the case is?"

"I'm a friend of Iris's family. I live across the street from her grandniece. They invited me to the family seder on Passover this year, and afterwards they told me how Aunt Iris had disappeared from a seder a long time ago. I've had some experience investigating homicides unofficially and very unprofessionally, and the family asked me if I would look into this. I'm not very optimistic because it happened so long ago and no one has anything to go on, but I thought I'd give it a try. I met my husband while I was looking into my first homicide."

"Jack Brooks?"

"Yes."

"Greg told me about him. Says he's a real nice guy."

"Well, I think so."

Harris smiled. "I'm sure he is. OK. You want to look over the file, ask me questions—?"

"Both, actually. Why don't I ask first so you can get back to work while I look at the file."

"At your disposal."

"Who found the body?"

"Coupla kids with a dog."

"That was a day and a half or so after she disappeared, is that right?"

"Just about."

"What was the estimated time of death?"

"The ME felt she'd been killed sometime during the night she disappeared."

"Was she wearing her jewelry?"

"We weren't sure it was all there. Everyone in the family remembered something different. She had her watch and a ring that her relatives said she always wore, and there may have been a bracelet—I'd have to check—but some of them thought she'd been wearing a gold pin and some of them thought she'd had a gold chain on. But it didn't look like a robbery."

"How did she die, Harris?"

"He used his hands and fists and feet on her. There was no indication of any weapon. Basically, he beat her to death."

"Is that unusual?"

"People kill in a lot of different ways, but I would

say this is the way that shows anger, retribution, revenge. If you go out to kill someone, you take a weapon with you. I'd almost guess this was a case where she got him angry to the point where he lost control."

"Someone in the family thinks she may have promised to lend someone some money. Maybe she didn't bring it with her or maybe she didn't bring enough, and that set him off."

"Could be, but we couldn't find anyone like that. Most of the neighbors never heard of her, her family all seemed on very good terms with her—they didn't talk about each other behind their backs—and we really couldn't find anyone with a grudge."

"How about the people she worked with? According to her niece, Iris worked on Park Avenue for a man named Wilfred Garganus."

"No, that's not true."

"I beg your pardon?"

"She wasn't working there anymore. She'd left about a week before she died."

"Did she quit?"

"That wasn't clear. I interviewed and reinterviewed people in and away from that office myself. I always had the feeling they knew something that they didn't want to tell me. For the record, she left voluntarily. Me, I didn't think it was so voluntary. But I never got anyone to say otherwise."

"I'm really surprised about that. As far as her family's concerned, she'd been working there for years and she was still working there the day she died."

"Either they don't know or they don't want to tell you."

"Do you have the name of the company?"

"Sure." He looked through some papers and pulled one out. "GAR, Inc. Some multinational corporation. Their headquarters were at 102 Park Avenue, but I can tell you they're not there anymore. They moved to Long Island about ten years ago. But it's possible they've left some of their corporate staff in that building. You want to talk to them?"

"I was told her boss, Mr. Garganus, died some years ago, but if there was anyone who remembered her, I'd really like to talk to them. Do you mind?"

"Not at all. Just so long as you let me know if you learn anything."

"That's a promise. One more thing. Did you learn anything about boyfriends or men she went out with?"

"There was someone. Hold on." He made a quick search and said, "She'd had like a steady boyfriend at one time, a Harry Schiff. It was a little touchy interviewing him. He had a wife, had her all the time he was seeing Iris Grodnik."

"That was my impression, too. I guess you didn't think he was a suspect."

"Didn't seem like it to me. He was really broken up about Iris. He cried when we talked. He told me he'd been in love with her for years, but she broke up with him because he couldn't or wouldn't divorce his wife. He was a man in his sixties, struck me as a nice guy. I had to consider him, of course, but I didn't seriously think he'd killed her."

"Did you hear anything about a newer boyfriend?"

"Nothing we could track down. You know something I don't know?"

"Iris's sister said there was a new man in Iris's life. She has no name. I just wondered if you did."

"Sorry."

"I suppose you checked out her finances, whether she was paying money to anyone or getting money from anyone besides her employer?"

"She got her check from the company every week and made her own deposits. She usually didn't deposit the whole thing, but who does? Was she paying anyone blackmail? Not by check, she wasn't. Did she have any mysterious income we couldn't account for? Didn't look like it. She had some savings, some investments, some interest. Anything else I can tell you?"

"Let me look at the file for a while. I can always get back to you afterwards."

"Sure thing. There's an empty desk right over there. Make yourself comfortable."

"Thanks."

I spent the rest of the morning looking at the file. There were some ugly pictures of Iris's body that I only glanced at and then turned facedown. The autopsy report was pretty technical, but I gathered she had died the way Harris White had described. Then there were the interviews with people who lived in her building, most of whom had never heard of her till she died. The next-door neighbor, a single woman in her thirties, had known and liked Iris. They didn't socialize, but they chatted with each other, sometimes dropped in on each other in the evening. If there had been a boyfriend, Miss Able wasn't aware.

Wilfred Garganus, the man for whom Iris had worked for so many years, gave a long interview, but he was vague about Iris's reasons for leaving. He said there was a chance she might come back, that she was thinking of doing some traveling, that she had some personal problems she wanted to take care of. He was shocked and saddened by the news of her death and wanted the family to know he would contribute to any memorial they established in her memory. Whether he ever told this to the family was a mystery to me. Marilyn certainly had never referred to such a gesture. There were also a couple of interviews with neighbors of Abraham Grodnik, people who might have seen Iris leave the apartment during the fateful seder, but none of them had.

Finally there was a brief interview with Shirley Finster. It was done by telephone, apparently initiated by Shirley, who called the police to inquire about her friend's case. She gave no address and no phone number, and it appeared that she hung up when she decided she'd answered enough questions. The ones she did answer gave me nothing new. She had known Iris since they were children, they loved each other like sisters, she couldn't imagine who would do such a thing to such a wonderful person. No, she hadn't seen Iris for a while, but that was because Shirley had moved and they had both been very busy. And that was it. All in all a tough case with few leads, and those pretty cold now after so many years.

Harry Schiff's address was in the West Seventies, hence Aunt Sylvie's mistaken belief that he lived near Abraham. I wrote it down and also the name of Iris's next-door neighbor, with little hope of finding her still there, and then borrowed a Manhattan phone book and looked up GAR. Sure enough, there was a listing at

102 Park Avenue. I turned to the *S*'s and found an
H. Schiff at the address Harry had lived at when Harris
White interviewed him. It wasn't much, but it was a
start. I thanked the detective, promised again he would
hear if I learned anything, and was on my way.

11

102 Park Avenue was right near Forty-second Street, the wrong part of New York to find an inexpensive garage, so I left the car a bit uptown and a bit east and walked back, stopping for lunch on the way. I had still not gotten over my surprise that Iris had left her job a week before the murder. Why hadn't she told the family? If she was planning to retire, or to take a kind of sabbatical, why would she keep that a secret? I wondered if that was the secret Sylvie had mentioned, the one no one else in the family would tell me. It didn't make sense. But the very fact that there were unexplained quirks in Iris's life made her interesting and gave me cause to look into her murder.

The building was old, but the elevators were new and arranged in banks, each going to a different set of floors. GAR was on seven, and the first bank serviced the first ten floors. The elevator went up so quickly and so smoothly that I didn't know it had stopped till the door opened. The GAR suite was just down the carpeted hall, and I went inside to a quiet, softly lighted reception area that was empty except for an attractive young woman at a desk with a telephone and little else, and some guest chairs.

"May I help you?"

"I have kind of a strange reason for being here. A woman who worked in this office for many years was murdered about sixteen years ago, and I wondered if anyone from that time might still be around."

"Are you a relative of hers?"

"My name is Christine Bennett and I'm a friend of the family."

"Uh, what exactly do you want?"

A question not easy to answer. "I think I'd just like to talk to anyone who knew her."

She frowned a very pretty frown. "Let me get Mrs. Holloway, our office manager. Maybe she can help." She used the telephone, then told me to have a seat.

The chairs were grouped like benches. I had hardly had time to get comfortable when a woman appeared soundlessly.

"Miss Bennett?"

"Yes. Hi."

"I'm Mrs. Holloway. How may I help you?"

"I'm looking for anyone in this office who might remember Iris Grodnik. She worked here about—"

"I knew Iris." She was all smiles. "I knew Iris very well. Who are you?"

"I'm a friend of the family and I'm trying to find out whatever I can about Iris's death."

She turned to the receptionist and said, "Hold my calls." Then, to me, "Come with me. There's an empty conference room and I'll get us some coffee."

A few minutes later we were seated in one of those rooms with a long table and a lot of chairs on little wheels. A pitcher of coffee and some doughnuts were on a tray, and I felt relaxed and welcome.

"I haven't thought about Iris for a long time," Mrs. Holloway said. She was a nice-looking young woman, perhaps in her late thirties, wearing glasses and a black suit with a large silver pin on the lapel. "But I loved her when she was here. She was Mr. Garganus's secretary, the kind he couldn't have run the company without, but she was very down-to-earth. You know how some executive secretaries are; they think they're chief executive and they won't give you the time of day. Iris was a real person."

"How long did you know her?"

"About three years. She'd been here much longer than that, of course, ten or fifteen years anyway, but I was here for three when she died."

"Do you know anyone who worked here at that time who was getting married and could have had a bridal shower, someone whose name started with *C*?"

Her face lit up. "That's me," she said excitedly. "That was my shower. I'm Cathy. Iris was invited—the whole office was invited. How did you know about that?"

"It was in her engagement book. Believe it or not, the book just turned up last Friday."

"Oh my goodness. After all these years. Yes, I've been married a long time. We just had our sixteenth anniversary. We have two kids now. But Iris died before the shower."

"That's what I thought. Cathy, I have to ask you something that's been bothering me. According to the police, Iris left her job here a week or so before she died. Did you know that?"

"I knew it, yes."

"Do you know why?"

"That's not an easy question. The short answer is no, I don't know why Iris left."

"But there's a longer answer."

"There is, yes. The trouble is, I don't really know the whole story, and pretty much everything I could tell you would be secondhand."

"Tell me what you know, what you think, what you heard, anything you can dig up in your memory. I know that Mr. Garganus is dead and I'm not likely to find many more people—maybe not any more people—who remember her. The case is at a dead end and her family really wants to know what happened to her."

"She had a wonderful job here, the best job she could have had without being involved in the core work of the company. As far as I knew, she was a crack secretary. She'd been Mr. Garganus's private secretary for years, and he relied on her for everything. I think he replaced her with two people and was never happy with them even though they were good."

"Did she seem happy in her job?"

"She was a happy person. She didn't complain, unless it was on Mr. Garganus's behalf. Then she was a killer. If someone promised to mail him something and it didn't arrive, she was on the phone threatening them the minute she finished going through the mail. But she was a sweet, generous, friendly person. When my wallet was stolen one morning on my way to work, Iris handed me ten dollars and asked if that would be enough. That's the way she was."

"I can see why she was so well liked. Did everyone feel that way?"

"People are people. There were women who envied her her job, who thought she was overpaid, who thought she was snooty, but what can you do? Some people are just born jealous. I think Iris earned whatever she was paid, and that includes bonuses. She worked very hard and she put the company first."

"All of this sounds as though she had a job for life. Did something happen to change all that?"

"If anything happened, I didn't see or hear it. All I know for sure is that one Friday afternoon a notice came around that Iris Grodnik was leaving GAR for what they called an extended sabbatical."

"Did that mean she was coming back?"

"It was very vague. Personally, I thought she was retiring and Mr. Garganus was trying to get her to reconsider. But as well paid as she was, I don't see how she could have afforded to retire at that point. She was too young for Social Security, she was too young to pick up the company pension."

"Maybe she was thinking of getting married."

"I thought of that myself. But I had no way of knowing. Iris was very private about her personal life. She kept pictures on her desk of nieces and nephews, grandnieces and grandnephews, but you never knew if she had a boyfriend, if she lived a lonely single life, if she had been married—it was all a mystery."

"What was the office scuttlebut?"

Cathy Holloway looked unhappy. She took a breath and poured herself more coffee. "The vixens in the office said she'd been having an affair with Mr. Garganus for years, that his wife had finally found out about it and had given him an ultimatum."

"Do you think she was?"

"You have to remember that what I thought of Iris was colored by my feelings about her. She was nice to me. I liked her. I was young and kind of innocent. I thought Iris was a very moral person and I couldn't believe she'd have something going with her married boss."

"Now that a lot of time has passed and you're less innocent, do you think it may have happened?"

"I still think she was a moral person."

It was interesting to me that she felt that way. The story about Iris and Harry was that she didn't want to live with him if he didn't divorce his wife. That she had surely committed adultery said that Iris was a somewhat less moral person than Cathy gave her credit for, but ultimately she hadn't wanted a permanent relationship with a married man.

"I take it you never caught them in what might be considered an intimate moment?"

"Never. And no one else did either, I can assure you, or they would have splashed it all over the office. It's just that a couple of the women talked."

"So there was no prior notice to her leaving, no big party to say good-bye."

"Nothing like that, which was kind of unusual. Iris said she didn't want it. She told us she'd see us all at my shower and she left that Friday afternoon as if she were coming back the next Monday morning. Except, of course, that she didn't."

"And she died a violent death about a week later."

"I can't tell you how shocked we were when we heard it. It touched us all. It sounded like she went out for a walk or was on her way home and somebody grabbed her."

"I know that's the way it sounded, but it didn't happen that way," I said. "She left her brother's apartment without her pocketbook."

"I didn't know that."

"Nobody did. We just found her pocketbook last Friday, stuck in a corner of the closet where she put it to get it out of the way. It had her wallet and keys in it. You don't go home without your wallet and keys."

"So that means—"

"It means either that she went out to meet someone briefly or that she stepped out for a breath of fresh air, planning to return. Do you have any idea who she might have met that night?"

Cathy shrugged. "Not the slightest. As I said, I knew very little about her personal life."

"Do you know where Mr. Garganus lived at that time?"

She looked at me with eyes that showed surprise and fear. "I—I'm not sure."

"Could you find out?"

"I don't know. I . . . He lived on the East Side, somewhere in the East Seventies, I think. I seem to remember that he had lived in a big apartment, and when I was still fairly new here, he and his wife bought a town house."

"I see."

"In fact, I think Iris may have gone there once or twice to deliver something. It's a long time ago and I don't really remember very clearly, but I think she said it was very beautiful and Mrs. Garganus was decorating it magnificently."

"Do you know if Mrs. Garganus is still alive?"

"I haven't heard that she died. I think I would have."

"Do you know about how old Mr. Garganus was

when Iris died, or how old he would be now if he had lived?"

"He was a very good-looking man," Cathy said. "Kind of the classic CEO with silver hair and a trim body. He was probably older than he looked, and I would guess he was a little older than Iris. I think she was in her late fifties, although she could easily have passed for less, and he was probably in his early sixties."

"So he was close to retirement."

"He was, yes. In fact, he did retire a few years after she died."

"Did they keep the town house?"

"I believe so."

"Could you get me the address, Cathy?"

She smiled sadly. "How did I know that question was coming? I could. I know where to find it. I'm just not sure—"

"There was a murder," I said solemnly. "That case has been open for sixteen years. I really want to know who killed that poor woman. If Mrs. Garganus could tell me something that could lead in the right direction, it would really be very helpful."

She sat staring at the blank wall as though making a life-and-death decision. "I'll do it," she said finally, "but you must promise that my name will never be associated with the information I'm going to give you."

"You have my word."

"Anything else before I go to the file?"

"Iris had a lifelong friend named Shirley Finster. I haven't been able to find any reference to her anywhere, not in the engagement book, not on any notes in the pocketbook. No one seems to know where she lived, if she's married, anything. Does the name ring a bell for you?"

"I do remember that Iris had a friend, a woman friend, that she talked about. Maybe the name was Shirley, but I couldn't swear to it. I don't know anything else about her."

"Are any other people from that group still around?"

"The older women have all retired, and one or two of them have died. One of the younger women moved out to Long Island when the company bought a headquarters building out there several years ago. To tell you the truth, I can't remember her last name. I'd say I'm your best source, and it's very lucky that the receptionist called me. I don't think there's another person in this building who remembers Iris."

"Thank you."

"Stay here. It'll just take a minute."

She left the room, closing the door behind her. I leaned back luxuriously in my chair, wondering if its comfort spelled a reason why so many conferences were held in large corporations. It certainly felt good. Maybe all those legendary meetings were groups of people needing a short nap and good back support.

It took about five minutes for Cathy Holloway to return. She gave me a smile as she came in, sat beside me, and handed me an address on a piece of plain white paper.

"It's Seventy-fourth Street," she said. "I don't know if they'll let you in and I couldn't find a telephone number either in the file or in the phone book. I'm not surprised that it's unlisted."

I wasn't either. I looked at the address. The number appeared to be in approximately the same block as

Abraham Grodnik's apartment house, and three blocks north. A man could walk those three blocks easily in five minutes, six or seven if he chose to take his time.

"Will you go there to see her?" Cathy asked.

"I think I have to."

"Well, good luck."

I thanked her and said I was sure I would need it.

12

Since my car was already parked, I went out on Park Avenue and hailed a cab. I looked out the window as we drove north. Park is one of the most elegant streets in New York, divided with a green strip in the center that is decorated for Christmas with lights and planted with colorful flowers in the spring and summer. The apartment houses are quietly genteel and speak of the finest things that money and good taste can buy. Uniformed doormen mark the entry of each one, well-dressed men and women—and dogs—parade up and down in front of them, limousines load and unload the wealthiest and most well-known people in the country.

At Seventy-fourth Street the taxi turned right. "You goin' to an embassy or somethin'?" the driver asked.

"It's a private home."

He whistled. "Pretty nice place to live."

I thought so myself. The New York town house was a style made for the wealthy who chose not to live in a Park Avenue apartment. Narrow and four or five stories tall, they stood shoulder to shoulder along the cross streets of the city, some with fancy wrought-iron gates and entrances, others almost quietly retiring. I had never been in one and had no idea what to expect, but I occasionally hear of one being sold for millions of dollars, a far cry from anything in little Oakwood.

"This the one?" the driver asked.

I checked the address in my hand. "Yes it is." I paid him and got out, suddenly feeling a little nervous. I knew I had little chance of being admitted, less of being welcomed. But I kept thinking of how close this house was to the site of that fateful seder, a pleasant walk. And then what? Come to my car, I want to show you something?

I went up to the door and rang the bell. I heard the sound of the chimes inside, but nothing else. I waited. What kind of a car would he have had? A big black Mercedes with almost enough power to fly to the tip of Manhattan? I rang the bell again, thinking I had surely made this little trip in vain.

"I'm on my way," a voice called, a young, female voice. It wasn't what I expected.

Then the door opened and she stood before me, a pretty girl in her teens, blue jeans, an enormous sweater, and a peaches-and-cream complexion with very blue eyes. "Hi," she said with a smile. "Are you lost?"

"I don't think so. I'm looking for Mildred Garganus."

"She's my grandmother. Come on in. She expecting you?"

"I'm not sure," I said, so surprised at being inside without a long explanation that I truly wasn't sure.

"She's upstairs. Come on, we can walk."

As though I had expected to fly. "I'm Christine Bennett." We started up a beautiful staircase with a dark, polished banister. There were paintings along the wall as we climbed, above them lights that had gone on when the girl flicked a switch.

"I'm Erin Garganus. Gram?" she called. "Christine Bennett is here. I'm bringing her up."

"Who?" a woman's voice called back.

"Christine Bennett."

I followed her into a room at the back of the house, a beautiful second-story living room with almost floor-to-ceiling glass at the rear wall. Sitting near the window was a woman in a wheelchair. As I saw her, I knew I didn't want to do what I had come for.

"Who exactly did you say you were?"

"My name is Christine Bennett, Mrs. Garganus. I'm a friend of the family of Iris Grodnik."

"Oh, for heaven's sakes. Erin, don't you ask people what they're here for before you let them in?"

The girl shrugged. "She looked OK to me."

"Go to your room and lie down, Erin. When Elena comes, she'll make you a cup of cocoa. Erin thought she had a cold this morning, so she stayed home from school," she explained to me. "Go on, Erin. I can take care of this."

I watched the girl go, continuing up the stairs with a prance. "She's lovely," I said.

"She's a handful," Mrs. Garganus said. She had been sitting so she could look out the window on the garden below. Now she turned to face me. "We can take the elevator down, Miss Bennett, is it? I will show you out."

"If you could just give me a few minutes, Mrs. Garganus."

"I know nothing about that woman. There is nothing I can tell you. My late husband was interviewed by the police at the time it happened, and I'm sure he knew much more about it than I possibly could." She started rolling her chair toward what I realized was an elevator.

"Did you ever meet Miss Grodnik?" I asked.

"Once or twice. Sometimes she had to bring things from the office for my husband. She was a nice woman. She worked for my husband for a long time. She was probably the best secretary he ever had."

"I'm told she quit a week before she was murdered."

Mrs. Garganus cocked her head to look at me. "I wouldn't know. I left the business end of things to my husband."

"Did you like her?"

"That's really a very stupid question," she said irritably. "If I hardly knew her, how could I like or dislike her?"

The elevator was right there and I wanted to keep her talking so that she wouldn't open the door and end the conversation forever. She was a very pretty woman, dressed as though she were on her way to lunch or tea, bracelets on her wrists, rings on her fingers, a gold pin with little diamonds on the wool dress she was wearing. Her tart tongue made her seem older than she looked. She might have been only seventy.

"There seems to have been something strange about her leaving GAR," I said.

"There was nothing strange about it at all. She wanted to do some traveling, she wanted to have some fun while she was young enough and strong enough to do it. You never know what disagreeable problems age can bring with it."

"Where was she planning to go?" I asked.

"Europe somewhere. I think Switzerland. Switzerland's a beautiful country. We used to go there."

"She never mentioned this trip to her family."

"My dear young woman, I cannot be responsible for what someone does or does not tell her family. I'm sure when the appropriate time came, she would have told them."

She pulled the elevator door open, and I held it as she rolled into it. It was small but large enough to accommodate the two of us. She pushed the 1 button and the elevator lurched downward. On the main floor, I opened the door and got out, waiting for her to follow.

"Your granddaughter looks just like you," I said. It was true, but I was trying desperately to keep the conversation going, to say something that would make her open up.

"Thank you. I take that as a compliment. She's a very pretty girl and she looks exactly as I did when I was her age; not the way she dresses, of course. The charm of the ubiquitous blue denim of young people is lost on me."

"They're comfortable," I said as we moved toward the front door. "And she has such a lovely figure."

"With all the junk she eats it's a wonder. What did you say your name was?"

"Christine Bennett." I dug in my bag for a slip of paper, wrote my name, address, and phone number on it and handed it to her. "If you think of anything else, Mrs. Garganus, please give me a call. The family really wants to know what happened to Iris. The police have been at a dead end for years. I believe she was killed by someone who knew her; I don't think it was a random killing."

She looked up at me. "What makes you think that?"

"We just found her handbag in a closet last Friday.

When she went out that night, she went without her wallet, her keys, or her ID."

"That is curious. I'm sorry I can't think of anything that will help you."

"Thank you for your time."

"Incidentally, where did you get my address from?"

I was ready for that. "It was in Iris's address book."

"Really," she said.

"Good-bye, Mrs. Garganus."

I walked the rest of the way to Second Avenue—the house had turned out to be a block farther west than the Grodniks' apartment house—and hailed a cab to take me to my parking garage. I couldn't remember the last time I had been in two taxis in one day, much less in one hour, and my extravagance was giving me second thoughts. I remembered the first time I parked a car in New York and wondered if the fee was actually a monthly rental. Marilyn had promised to pay my expenses "and then some," and I had thanked her for the expenses and said the "then some" was quite unnecessary. I hoped she wouldn't think I was reckless.

The car was another small fortune, and as soon as I had paid it, I headed back to Oakwood. I felt I had learned a lot, more than I had hoped for.

When I got home, I called my sister-in-law.

"Oh, Chris, it's nice to hear from you. Jack told me you made an incredibly generous offer. I can't take it, but thanks so much."

"Think about it, Eileen. I have money just sitting in a bank account, doing no one any good. I'd like to see it do you some good."

"I really have to do this myself. I went to a couple of banks today and got the royal runaround. What I can't accept is that Taffy would do something like this, and to me."

"Maybe something was going on in her life that you didn't know about."

"Maybe so. She sure isn't going to retire on twelve thousand dollars. I keep wondering if I did something to hurt her, if she was trying to get back at me for something."

"Eileen, I'm sure you didn't. I don't think you should waste one second of your life worrying about something like that. You're an honest, generous person. Whatever caused Taffy to do this, it came from her."

"Thanks, Chris." She sounded choked up.

"And don't forget my offer. Forget the banks. Whatever you need is right here."

She said she'd think about it.

Jack got home at his usual late hour, having gone to his classes. I warmed up the stew I had planned for Friday night and sat with him in the kitchen as he ate.

"How's Greg Jarvis?" he asked.

"I didn't see him. But I had a good talk with Harris White. He's very nice and very anxious to close the case. It was one of his first."

"Right. When you think you're a super sleuth."

"That's the way it sounded. I learned a lot, Jack, more than I ever expected."

"I'm listening."

"Iris quit her job a week before she was murdered."

"And no one in the family told you?"

"I'm sure they didn't know. I called Marilyn when I

came home and told her, and she said it must be a mistake. But it isn't. I heard it from the detective, from someone who was working there at the time, and—" I paused dramatically "—from the wife of Iris's boss, the CEO of the company."

"You do get around. How'd you find her?"

"The woman at GAR gave me her address as long as I promised not to divulge my source. The house is three and a half blocks from where Iris was the night she disappeared. I taxied over, rang a bell, and her granddaughter answered. I gather from something Mrs. Garganus said that the maid would be along later. The granddaughter was a sweet kid who took me upstairs to see her grandmother."

"Not bad for a first try."

"You never told me about those town houses."

He grinned. "Nice, huh?"

"So many of them look so bleak from the outside and they're so narrow, I've often wondered how anyone could live there."

"Pretty nice when you get in."

"He must have been very rich. The furniture is fantastic, there's artwork all over the place, rugs that must have been handwoven. It's just that everywhere you go is upstairs or downstairs."

"That's how they were built, a room in the front, a room in the back. Did it have an elevator?"

"It did. Mrs. Garganus is in a wheelchair, so I guess it's the only way she could manage. And Jack, she said things that really show she knows a lot more about Iris than she said she did."

"Like what?"

"Well, we only talked a couple of minutes because

she spent the whole time I was there showing me out, but she started out by saying that she didn't know anything about Iris quitting her job, and a minute later she told me Iris was planning to travel, probably to Switzerland. I mean, it was as if she didn't remember what she'd just said."

"So either she had a personal relationship with Iris—"

"Which I don't think she would have."

"Or her husband discussed Iris with her."

"In detail, Jack. Not just that Iris wanted to travel but that she was going to Europe, probably to Switzerland. That woman knows something I want to know."

"You know me. I wouldn't bet against you."

"My problem is this. What I really want to know is whether Wilfred Garganus was having an affair with Iris, and I can't ask Mrs. Garganus that. It's a very insensitive thing to do, but I don't know how else I can find out."

"You think they were having an affair, Mrs. G. found out, and an agreement was made for Iris to quit her job and leave the country, kind of to let the affair simmer down."

"I think it's a possibility. But who would know except Mrs. G. at this point?"

"How 'bout her best friend?"

"That's another troublesome point." I described the interview in the file at the Thirty-fourth Precinct. "No address, no phone number. She sure didn't want to be contacted again."

"And the detective didn't try to find her."

"Not from anything I saw in the file. I don't exactly blame him. The way the body was beaten, it wasn't done by a woman of almost sixty. What could she know that would help the police?"

"Her secrets," Jack said. "She was a best friend, wasn't she?"

13

Tuesday morning I teach. I am still teaching "Poetry and the Contemporary American Woman" at a local college in Westchester, a job I truly enjoy. But on that Tuesday morning, I made a phone call before I left for the college. I dialed Harry Schiff's number.

A woman answered and made me jump through some hoops before she got him to the phone. But finally he picked up.

"Mr. Schiff, my name is Christine Bennett and I'm a friend of the family of Iris Grodnik."

"Oh my God," he said.

"I'd like to talk to you."

"I don't think so. I don't think I can."

"I can meet you wherever you want. I have a car. I could even pick you up."

"No, no, it's all over. It's gone. It's too long."

"It's really very important. I could see you this afternoon."

"Today? Oh, I don't know."

"What would be good for you?"

"I don't want to talk about it, I really don't."

It's so easy on the telephone to turn someone down. "Please, Mr. Schiff. We've found something of Iris's, something that was hidden away since she died. It would really help if I could talk to you."

"What did you find?"

"The pocketbook she had that night. She didn't have it with her when she left her brother's apartment."

"Oh my God."

"If we could just get together for a little while and talk."

"This is terrible," he said. "Look, all right, I'll do it. I shouldn't, but I will. I like to take a walk in the afternoon, but it's too cold to meet outside. There's a place, Vinny's, on Seventy-second Street between West End and Broadway. You know the area?"

"Very well."

"Vinny's. On the south side of the street. I'll be there at—when can you meet me?"

"Two-thirty."

"Two-thirty is good. I'll be there at two-thirty. What do you look like?"

That's a question I can never answer. I looked down at what I was wearing. "I'll be wearing a black raincoat and carrying a briefcase."

"I'll look for you. I'll get a table for two. This afternoon, right?"

"Right."

"Good-bye."

I had a light, tasty lunch in the college cafeteria when my class was over and then drove into the city. About halfway there it started to rain and I wondered if Harry Schiff would make it to Vinny's. I knew the area because an elderly friend of mine had lived and been murdered in a building in the West Seventies and I had visited a number of apartments around there, about a year and a half ago, looking for leads. I drove down Riverside Drive and found a place to park not far from Seventy-second Street and then walked over the block and a half till I found Vinny's. It was just two-thirty when I closed my umbrella and went inside.

It had the look of a neighborhood hangout for the elderly. At one table four men were playing cards. Besides the cards there were four cups of coffee on the table and nothing else. At another table two men played chess, again with mugs of coffee beside them. I wondered how poor Vinny made a living. As I looked around, a man rose from a table for two and looked at me. I walked over.

"Mr. Schiff?"

"That's me."

"Hi. I'm Christine Bennett."

"Sit down. What can I get you?"

"Coffee would be fine."

"The cheesecake is good."

"OK."

"Mike," he called to a nearby waiter, "two coffees, two cheesecakes."

"Comin' up, Mr. Schiff."

"What do you have to do with Iris?" he asked.

As Marilyn had said, he was a tall, nice-looking man, now completely gray and I guessed near eighty. He had dressed for our meeting, a white shirt, a blue silk tie. I wondered how often he put on clothes like these to take his afternoon walk.

"I know her grandniece. I was invited to their seder this year and they told me about Iris."

"It was terrible, a tragedy. I never got over it."

"They asked me to try to find out who killed her."

"You think in a city like this you can find out who killed a woman sixteen years ago when the police couldn't do it?"

"I'm giving it a try. Tell me about yourself, Mr. Schiff."

He gave me a smile. "I'm a retired accountant. I met Iris so many years ago I can't even remember; it must have been in the fifties. She was beautiful, she was sweet, she was a little angel."

"Everyone who knew her says nice things about her."

"You couldn't say anything else. I was crazy about her. But back then, forty years ago, things were a lot different. I had kids at home, I was a professional man, you had to live a certain way. You know what I'm saying?"

"I understand."

"Later on, when my children got older, I moved out for a while and lived by myself. We had a good time together, Iris and me. I'm sure you're smart enough to figure out I don't get along with my wife, but divorce is a big step, it's not always easy. She made threats, she said she'd tie me up in court for years, and she could have done it. Finally Iris said, 'Either we get married or it's over.' I couldn't believe it would ever be over, but she meant it. I gave up my apartment and went back to my wife."

"How long before Iris died did you stop seeing her?"

"It was a few years. I can't tell you exactly."

"Did you keep in touch?"

"Well, you know, a telephone call now and then, some flowers on her birthday. I didn't forget her, if that's what you mean, and I don't think she ever forgot me."

"Did she keep you current on her life?"

"We talked. She told me this one got married, that one had a baby."

"What about her job? Did she talk about that?"

"She had a wonderful job, worked for a wonderful man. She loved it."

"Did you ever meet her boss?"

"Mr. Garganus? How would I ever meet him?"

"I just thought—maybe when you were still going with her—you might have . . ." I let it dangle, hoping he would fill in something I could use.

"I never saw the man in my life."

"Do you remember the last time you saw Iris?"

"Like it was yesterday. I called and asked her if I could take her out for her birthday. That was in December. She was fifty-nine. I took her to a beautiful restaurant, I sent her flowers to her apartment. We had a wonderful time."

"So it was several months before she died."

"Yeah, it was a long time."

"Mr. Schiff, this is hard for me. I'd like to ask you—do you know if Iris was seeing anyone else after you and she stopped, uh, keeping company?"

"Another man?"

"Yes."

"She never told me. Who was he?"

"I don't know that she was seeing anyone. I just wondered if she was, if you knew whether she was."

"Nah, I don't think so. You think she was?"

I felt terrible discussing something so obviously painful to him, something that may never have happened. "I truly don't know," I said. "Uh, let me throw something kind of wild out and see what you think. Do you think she could have been seeing her boss?"

"Iris going out with Mr. Garganus? Never."

"You never had a sense—when you broke up with her, you never thought it might be because there was another man? That she might be interested in Mr. Garganus?"

"Never. We were in love. We had a thing going twenty-five years. That's longer than most people stay married nowadays. No, I gotta tell you, we belonged together. I think when we broke up she was hoping maybe it wasn't too late to find someone and settle down, but I don't think she had the someone at that time. And I don't think Mr. Garganus was ever a possibility."

"When you took her out for her birthday, did she mention that she was going out with anyone?"

"Not a word."

"Mr. Schiff, can you think of anyone Iris knew whose name begins with *M*?"

"First name or last name?"

"Either one."

"Lemme see."

The coffee and cheesecake had come, and he sipped his coffee and rubbed his forehead. "I knew her niece, Marilyn. That's one."

"Yes."

"You want another?"

"If you can think of any."

"I can't. Unless . . ."

"Yes?"

"I shouldn't tell you. She wouldn't like it. What do you need this for anyway?"

"We found her little engagement book in her handbag. She had the seders written in, and under the second one was an *M*. Maybe she changed her mind and decided to see *M* during the first seder. When she left her brother's apartment that night, she left her bag behind, which meant she intended to return. So it's possible she went outside to meet someone."

"For what?"

"I don't know. But if I could find the person she met, we might have her killer."

"I see. And the police never found this guy?"

"The police never saw her pocketbook till yesterday morning when I gave it to them."

"You found it?"

"Yes." It was too complicated to bring Marilyn into the picture. It was hard enough to get this man to answer my questions without asking two or three of his own.

"How do you like that?"

"What is it you were going to tell me?"

"Well, I suppose it's OK. She's gone a long time now."

"A very long time."

"Before I met her, when she was in her twenties maybe, she got married."

"I see."

"I didn't know her then. She told me when we were going out. She could understand the trouble I was having with my wife because she'd had a pretty tough time of it herself. With her it didn't last long. With me it was my whole life."

"Do you know the name of her husband?"

"She must've told me. I don't know. You hear something forty years ago, it's not so easy to remember."

"Think about the *M*."

"Murray, Max, Manny, Milton. Doesn't ring a bell."

"I wonder if-her sister knows."

"Sylvie? How's Sylvie doing? She's a sweet girl."

I smiled. That sweet girl was at least eighty. "She's fine. She was at the seder I went to a few weeks ago. My feeling is they were very close."

"They were. Iris was everyone's favorite."

"Did Iris have any children, Mr. Schiff?"

"Nah. They weren't married that long. He was a real no-goodnik. She went to Reno and got a divorce."

"Reno?"

"In those days you couldn't get a divorce in New York State. So if you had the money, you went to Reno for six weeks, said you were living there as a resident, and they'd give you a divorce. They had a whole industry there, people staying in cheap hotels, spending all the money they had saved, just to get a divorce. When the law changed here, that was the end of Reno."

"I guess I don't know much about divorce law," I said.

"Better not to."

I took out a piece of paper and wrote my name, address, and phone number on it. "If you think of Iris's husband's name, would you call me?"

"Sure. It's just I gotta do it from a pay phone. Too many questions if my wife sees a long-distance call on the bill. I'm the one should've gone to Reno. I wasn't as smart as Iris."

"I'm sure you did the right thing, Mr. Schiff. Your

children must appreciate that they came from a home with two parents."

"It's hard to tell sometimes what they appreciate, but my kids are pretty good to me. Anything else I can tell you?"

"Who would have killed Iris?"

"Nobody on the face of this earth."

I hadn't expected much else. "Mr. Schiff, I learned something rather strange yesterday. Did you know that Iris had quit her job about a week before she disappeared?"

"Quit her job? No. Why would she do that?"

"She never told you she was planning to quit?"

"That I would remember. She never told me."

"Did you talk to her after the birthday dinner?"

"I'm sure I must've. I called her maybe once a month. That can't be true. She would've told me."

I ate the last bite of cheesecake and finished my coffee. It had been a long conversation and I had the feeling I had told him more than he had told me, except that Iris had been married, which was certainly news. "I think that's about it," I said. "It's been very nice meeting you. I hope you'll call if you think of anything that could help."

"If I think of anything, you'll hear from me."

"My car is parked on Riverside Drive. If you can walk a couple of blocks, I can take you home."

"Nah," he said. "I like to walk in the rain. It reminds me of Iris."

I kind of smiled on the way home. It's a cliché to say I'll never understand people, but like most clichés, it's true. My personal feelings on marriage and divorce aside, I could not see what could have bound this man so firmly to a wife he professed to dislike that he could not disengage himself for the woman he loved and who apparently loved him. People make strange concoctions of their lives, and Harry Schiff had to be a champion. He had spent twenty-five years loving one woman while married to another, and he surely would have spent the rest of his life the same way if she hadn't stopped him. I wondered if something special had made her give him the ultimatum, whether it was, indeed, another man in her life (and she was too sweet to want to hurt Harry by telling him) or if it was just the power of the quarter-century mark, a woman asking herself whether it had all been worth it. I didn't think I would ever find an answer.

I got home a little before five and saw the answering machine blinking at me. I pressed the button while I took my wet coat off.

"Hi, hon. Don't bother making anything for me to eat tonight. There's a party at the house and I'll eat enough to keep me happy. A cup of coffee would be appreciated, though. See you later." That, of course, had been my Jack. "Chris, this is Cathy Holloway. I was intrigued by some of the things we talked about yesterday and I did a little digging this morning and found something I think will interest you. Give me a call and I'll tell you about it."

I looked at my watch, then scrambled to find Cathy's phone number. The receptionist answered and said it was too late to put me through, but finally said she'd ring the number.

"Mrs. Holloway."

"Cathy, this is Chris Bennett. I just got home and heard your message. Are you on your way out?"

"No, that's all right. I have a minute or two. It's really very odd, what I found."

"Tell me."

"Well, you remember I mentioned that Iris was too young to get Social Security and too young for the company pension, so I didn't know how she'd manage. This morning I went into the old payroll files. We've always paid every Monday, and a check was sent to Iris the Monday after the Friday she announced she was leaving."

"That was for the previous week," I said.

"That's right. And that should have been her last check. If there was accumulated vacation, that would have gone out the same day. But there was no notation that I could find that she had left GAR. And sure enough, the following Monday, another paycheck went out to her."

"As though she was still working?"

"Exactly as if she was still working. It was a couple of days later that she disappeared and died. The Monday after that, we sent her a final check and a notation was made in the record that she was deceased."

"So the records look as if she never quit."

"That's right."

"Can you think of any reason why that would be?"

"The only reason I can think of is that she didn't quit at all. But for the life of me, I don't know what she was doing for GAR if she wasn't coming into the office."

"Thanks, Cathy. I don't understand it either, but I'll see if I can figure it out."

"If I find anything else, I'll give you a call."

I thanked her, but she had already done more than I had hoped for.

14

"You make a good cup of coffee," Jack said, leaning back on the sofa. "You didn't learn that from me."

"Since I couldn't do anything else at St. Stephen's, they made me chief coffee maker—and taught me how to do it."

"Good enough. You make a damn good stew, too."

"Five nights a week."

He smiled. "Not quite. You know, I was thinking. We should put a family room on the house."

"Where?" I asked with some alarm.

"Out back, behind the kitchen."

"But I'd lose my windows and my view of the garden."

"You'd still have windows on the side, and we'd put the windows on the back of the family room so we could sit there and look out. And the light would still come into the kitchen."

"Let's think about it," I said uneasily.

"You worried about the cost?"

"A little." It was something I always worried about, and he knew it.

"Well, don't. The house'll be worth a lot more with the addition. And we'll love it."

"Let's think about it."

"Eileen said you called yesterday."

"Uh-huh."

"She thinks you're great."

"Well, I think she's pretty great. Didn't she give us the best wedding we could ever have had?"

"She did."

"She's a terrific person, and if I can help her, I want to."

"She's thinking about your offer."

"Good. I'm glad she didn't just reject it."

"What've you got for me tonight?"

I told him about Cathy Holloway's news.

"That's really interesting. So Iris quits, but she doesn't quit. Looks like she's on special assignment for her boss, doesn't it?"

"Like being his mistress?"

"Why not? You said yesterday his wife said Iris was going to take a trip. Maybe Garganus concocted a story for his wife, to put her off the trail. If the wife thinks Iris has left her job and gone around the world, she can stop worrying."

"So then what happens?" I picked up. "She mentions to him she'll be at her brother's for Passover, and he says he wants to see her and he'll walk over around eleven o'clock. She goes down to meet him and they have a fight."

"He couldn't have walked over," Jack said. "He would have had to drive over. I wonder if he had a driver."

"Even if he did, he could always drive the car himself if he felt like it."

"Possible," Jack said. He got up and came back with

a sheet of blank paper, folded it twice, and started to write notes on the short, folded edge. "Couple of things I don't like. One, he's not the kind of man who does the killing himself. I bet he was perfumed and manicured."

"His driver?"

"Could be." He made a note. "Chauffeurs know more about their bosses than wives do. Like partners on the job." He gave me a smile and patted my thigh. "Number two, I'm no expert on adultery, but this was a guy in his sixties, right?"

"Right."

"And a woman in her late fifties."

"Yes."

"When men get to be that age, don't they start looking at women in their twenties and thirties?"

"This was a very beautiful woman, petite and well dressed. She was charming and kind and a friend to everyone."

"OK, say I buy that. There's one more thing that doesn't fit. No way does Wilfred Garganus have an *M* in his name."

"But the *M* was on the day for the second seder. Whoever the *M* was that she was planning to meet, she died before she saw him."

"Or at the last minute he called and said he'd see her the first night. Well, we've got a lot more to work with now. You meet the old boyfriend today?"

"This afternoon. He's an awfully nice man, Jack, very tall for his age. You don't see many men around eighty over six feet tall. He's good looking and I think he got dressed up for me, shirt and tie. And it's pretty clear Iris was the great love of his life. If he has a flaw, it's that he could never bring himself to leave his wife.

Even now he doesn't enjoy living with her, but he does."

"It's called inertia."

"Whatever it's called, he knows it's his failing. He told me one interesting thing that may develop. Iris was once married."

"Sounds good."

"A long time ago, like fifty years or more. She was divorced soon after she was married; at least that's what she told him. He says that she was the smart one. It's what he should have done. He thinks Iris told him the name of her husband, but he can't remember it."

"So we have another nameless suspect. I don't suppose you could narrow down when they were married."

"Late thirties or forties."

"Not my idea of narrow."

"I bet Marilyn doesn't even know Iris was married, but I bet her father and Aunt Sylvie do."

"If they know, then they know a name."

"I really don't want to talk to Marilyn's father, but maybe Sylvie will tell me. She said she knew something no one else would tell, and this could be it."

"And they kept all this stuff to themselves when the police questioned them after Iris's death." I could hear the disappointment in his voice.

"A divorce in the thirties or forties was a family catastrophe," I said.

"So was a murder."

It was a little too late to argue the point with the Grodniks.

I called Marilyn early on Wednesday and said I had learned a lot and we should talk. She said she would be there in an hour. I spent the time cleaning up the kitchen and getting bags and bins ready for recycling. It's amazing how much we accumulate that we used to throw away, and Oakwood keeps telling us how much they're earning by collecting and selling all this material.

Marilyn pulled up the driveway and came to the door, carrying a shopping bag.

"Good morning," I said, opening the door before she rang.

"Chris, it's nice to see you. I have a little something for you and Jack."

The "little something" was a chocolate cake that smelled so good I knew I would have to restrain myself to keep it whole until tonight. "I guess Mel comes by it naturally."

"Oh, Mel is a much better cook than I am. I just gave her the impetus and she took off on her own." She took her coat off and hung it in the closet before I could take if from her. "Now, what's all this you've got for me?"

We sat in the living room, and for the first time I thought about what Jack had said last night, that it would be nice to build a family room behind the kitchen. I had to admit it would be a comfortable place to sit with a friend and chat, looking out over the garden with all that wonderful sunlight coming in.

"Did you know Iris was married when she was quite young?"

"Never heard a word. Are you sure about this?"

"I found Harry Schiff, Iris's old boyfriend, and had a long talk with him yesterday. She told him she'd been married, although I don't believe he or anyone else told the police. I bet your father knows all about it."

"I agree with you, but I don't think you should ask. Something's happened that I have to tell you about."

"Is he all right?"

"The same. It's not his health. I was talking to him on the phone and I told him we'd been to the apartment on Seventy-first Street. He blew up at me, Chris."

"I'm sorry," I said. "I certainly wouldn't have suggested we go there if I'd known it would upset him."

"I truly don't understand it. Maybe the illness is getting to him, although he said he was feeling all right. But he's decided to leave my sister's and go back to Seventy-first Street."

"Can he care for himself there?"

"I don't see how. I've been on the phone for the last twenty-four hours trying to get someone to live in. I think I've found a woman, someone from my town, who'll agree to go to New York for as long as she's needed. The whole thing is very upsetting. He'd be a lot better off at my sister's or at my house."

"Do you think he's doing this to keep us from snooping around?"

"I'm sure of it."

"I'm terribly sorry, Marilyn. The ripples are really spreading much wider than I ever expected. Why don't you tell him I have no intention of going into his apartment again?"

"I already promised him we'd keep away. He doesn't care. He wants to be there and that's it." She picked up some notes of mine that were lying on the coffee table in front of us. "Let's talk about Iris. Is that all Harry Schiff told you?"

"All that matters. But I've learned some other things

that may surprise you. I told you Iris quit her job at GAR more than a week before the Passover seder."

"And I still think that's impossible. Why would she quit? And if she did, she would have told us."

"Maybe she was intending to. I've seen the police file and talked to the detective on the case. The police knew she had quit."

"And they didn't tell us?"

"They interviewed Mr. Garganus and he told them. The detective probably didn't think there was anything unusual about it. People quit their jobs all the time and for one reason or another don't tell their families."

"She loved that job, Chris. It was her life."

"There's more to the story." I told her of my conversations with Cathy Holloway.

"So she quit and she didn't quit."

"That's the way it looks. I can't tell you why, and maybe there's no good reason, but I thought maybe she and Mr. Garganus had decided to take a little vacation together or get themelves a love nest somewhere."

Marilyn shook her head. "You're off base on that. I know it's easy to misjudge people we love, but I don't believe Iris ever thought of Mr. Garganus as anything but a wonderful man to work for."

"Be that as it may, I spoke to his wife."

"You *did*."

"I persuaded someone at GAR to give me the address, and his granddaughter opened the door and let me in. It was a stroke of luck. If the maid had been there, I would have been sent on my way."

"Well, thank goodness for small favors. What did you find out?"

"That she knows more than she will admit to. She

started out by saying she knew nothing about Iris and then she went on to tell me things no one in the family knew."

"Like what?" She was suddenly very interested.

"Like she said she didn't know Iris had quit her job and a minute later she was telling me that Iris wanted to travel to Europe—she mentioned Switzerland specifically—while she was still young enough to enjoy it."

"She told you that Iris was planning to go to Switzerland?"

"That's what she said."

"Iris didn't say a word. I wonder if she told my mother. She spent the whole afternoon cooking with her for Passover."

"Then your father would know."

"I'll have to ask him, if he's cooled down."

"Marilyn, it seems to me that after the kind of tragedy that happened to Iris, a family does a lot of second-guessing. If we had only known this, if we had only done that."

"We did it, Chris. After we knew she was dead, we sat shiva for a week."

"Excuse me?"

"After a death, the family mourns. In the old days the mourners actually sat on wooden crates, and I think we went out and found one for Pop. Nowadays they make special cartons with a design on the outside that makes it look like a wooden crate, like the old orange crates that you're too young to remember. When you mourn, you're not supposed to be comfortable. And each member of the immediate family tears a piece of clothing or wears a black ribbon that's been symbolically torn. Anyway, during that time, people visit the family—and plenty of people did—and the family comes together. I came in every day to be with Pop and Mom; my sister was there, my brothers came. And we went over and over what happened that night at the seder. We talked about Iris's life, her job, her apartment, her clothes, for heaven's sake. What could have happened that would make her end up a dead body in an oil yard? We took apart her life and her death. We got nowhere."

"And in all of that no one mentioned that she had been married?"

"Believe me, that's something I would remember. I told you, my parents' generation kept its secrets. Maybe when I wasn't there, maybe when only Sylvie was there, they talked about it. But you see, they never told the police. If they knew about it, and you're right, they probably did, they didn't think it was anyone's business, even the police investigating her murder."

"Marilyn, think about what happened after Iris's death. Did your father do anything unusual that you might be able to explain now that you know there was once a husband?"

"My father didn't do anything; my mother did. My mother and Sylvie cleaned out Iris's apartment. Pop wouldn't get involved in anything like that. Mom and Iris were close. They were sisters-in-law, but they were close. Pop loved her and she visited them a lot. He was the oldest and she the youngest, and he watched over her, all her life, I think."

"What did your mother do?" I prompted.

"She spent so much time at Iris's apartment we started to worry about her."

"It must have been a big job to clean it up."

"Well, it was, but it seemed more than that. I had the

feeling—how can I put it?—that she was fixing things up, arranging things, taking care of things."

"You said Iris didn't leave much money."

"Not enough to make someone want to kill her, and remember, what there was went to Melanie's generation. They were kids, young people. No one got rich on Iris's money, and no one would kill for her fur coat or gold necklace."

"This is very tough, Marilyn. We've got to find out who Iris's ex-husband was. If he's still alive, I want to talk to him. If he's dead, I want to know whether he died before or after Iris."

"I think we just have to ask Sylvie."

15

I sat across the kitchen table from Marilyn as she telephoned her aunt. With her usual warmth and manners, she started out asking how Sylvie was, inquiring about her health with attention to specific problems, the arthritis, the blood pressure, the difficulty walking. Gradually she shifted to a mention of me, to what a nice visit we had had last Friday. A couple of minutes went by in polite chitchat and then she said we had some other questions that had just come up that Sylvie could surely fill us in on.

I had my notebook open in front of me as Marilyn steered her aunt in the right direction.

"Sylvie, we've just heard something about Iris. Did you know she was once married?"

The answer was long and Marilyn said a lot of uh-huhs before she was able to repeat anything of value. "Nineteen thirty-nine? Really? She must have been very young." Slowly it emerged, a story buried in the older generation for half a century. Iris had married in the spring, in March, on the ninth or tenth, Sylvie thought, and brought her new husband home to her parents, who were so shocked and upset that they hardly knew what to say.

"Where did they live after they were married?" Marilyn asked innocently, and listened again for a long time. "Then she wasn't far from Grandma if she lived on the Concourse." The conversation went on as I waited. "What a shame," Marilyn said finally. "Then they weren't even married a year."

So Harry Schiff's information had been accurate. It had been a young, quick marriage that had not lasted. I tuned out most of the rest of the conversation, which got pretty boring as it drifted on to other things. Finally Marilyn said good-bye three times over a period of as many minutes and got off the phone.

"Poor thing," she said. "She's so alone. She's so happy to have someone call her. I was surprised she wasn't more hospitable Friday morning when we visited. I had the feeling she was almost throwing us out."

"Maybe it was too painful to talk about. She told me there was something she knew that no one else would tell me, but she wasn't ready to talk about it on Friday. I gave her my phone number, but she hasn't called yet. I expect this was it."

"Well, his name was Martin Handleman if that's any help."

"Martin," I said. "Iris had an *M* written on the page for the second seder in her book."

"I remember that. As though she were meeting someone whose name started with *M*. Maybe he called and said he'd see her the first night instead. Chris, this could be it."

"Maybe it is. Imagine harboring a grudge, a hatred, for forty years. It hardly seems possible."

"Anything's possible. For all we know, she was supporting him. Maybe that's how she got out of the marriage so quickly, by promising him money."

"That turns everything upside down, doesn't it?" I said. "Back then men were expected to support women during marriage and after marriage. Honestly, Marilyn, no woman would support a man for forty years on the basis of a marriage that lasted a few months."

"Then we'll find another theory. Where do we go from here?"

"Jack keeps a good supply of telephone books in the house. I'll go through all of them, the five boroughs, Westchester, and whatever else I can lay my hands on, and see how many Martin Handlemans I can find."

"There may be a lot. It's not an uncommon name."

"Then there are some other things. I'd like to see the marriage license; it'll give me some information on Martin Handleman. And there's one other thing." I stopped, feeling uneasy. "I don't mean to offend you, Marilyn, but it's possible Iris married to legitimize a child."

"No."

"I know it's hard to accept, and maybe I'm way off, but I don't believe people were that much different in 1939 from the way they are today. They may have kept their lives more private, but I doubt that sex was invented in the sixties."

Marilyn smiled. "You're right. It should be checked. I imagine that's going to be a massive job."

"I imagine so, too." I looked at my watch. "Let me call Arnold Gold. I think I could benefit from a nice chat with him."

"Go ahead. I'll be on my way. This is all turning out much more interesting and much more complicated than

I ever expected." She opened her bag and pulled out a wallet. "I know this is costing you a lot of money. Here's a down payment." She laid a hundred-dollar bill on the kitchen table.

I still palpitate a little when I see one of them. "Thank you. I'll keep a good accounting."

"Be generous to yourself. Have a good lunch on me. You deserve it."

I promised I would.

Arnold walked in as the secretary picked up my call.

"Chris?" he said, taking the phone from her. "How's things?"

"Interesting."

"What could be better? You want to come in and have some lunch with me? I just got an adjournment, so my day's not booked."

"I'd love it. It'll take me a little time to get there."

"I'm not in any rush. The restaurants I go to don't ask for a reservation."

"See you soon."

Arnold Gold rounds out my life. I live in a town that is a mixture of rich, middle class, and less than middle class, Protestants, Catholics, and Jews, well educated and not so well educated, Democrats and Republicans and a few little parties that I hear of only around election day, but the town tends toward the more well-to-do, the more educated, and the somewhat more conservative. Arnold Gold is a liberal. He defends people in every way you can imagine, and he does it with the enthusiasm of a person for whom there is nothing more exalted than the United States Constitution. He believes in it with his whole heart and soul and he defends it with fervor. Aside from the fact that he has become almost a second father to me, I admire and love him.

"Well, Chrissie," he said as I stepped inside the cluttered office that is his home base in downtown New York. "I've been so busy I haven't noticed whether you've been here or not."

"I finished up some work last week and got hooked into investigating an old homicide."

"How'd I guess? Don't sit down. We're on our way before that damn phone rings and ties me up for half an hour." He grabbed his coat and ushered me quickly out of the office before anyone could command his attention.

"It happened at a Passover seder," I said, and told him the story as we rode down the elevator and walked to the restaurant.

"So they found the body," he said as we sat down at a table. It was a pasta restaurant and we had been here before. "Remind me where these oil yards are."

"The northern tip of Manhattan. Jack says it's a great view if you're looking out, not so great if you're looking in."

"I suppose they cheat on the landscaping. Looks like she had a date with someone with a car."

"That's what we think."

"Although she could have taken a subway and gotten lost."

"She left her pocketbook behind."

"But you don't know what she had in her coat pocket. But OK, I grant you, if she left her bag behind, she probably got picked up by someone with a car."

"Right now I'm wondering if it might have been an ex-husband."

"Aha."

I filled him in on the rest. "When I get home, I'll start looking for Martin Handlemans in all the phone books in the metropolitan area."

"Good luck. I hope you can keep it down to twenty. You really think a man in his sixties did something like that to a woman?"

"Why not? You're in your sixties, aren't you? She was tiny. You could hold your own with a woman who weighed less than a hundred pounds, couldn't you?"

"I hope I could hold my own with a woman who weighed a lot more. I just don't know if I could kill her."

"Does age make it less likely that you'll kill?"

"Statistically, yes. Most of your killers are half my age. Which doesn't mean anything in the particular case we're talking about. Statistics only tell the big picture. Each crime is a very small part of that. What've you got on him?"

"Nothing except a name and the fact that they were married in March of 1939, probably the ninth. And divorced in Reno, but I'm not sure when."

"I tell you what. We're doing some digging of our own on an interesting case. If I throw in another marriage license, it won't make much of a difference to the guy who's doing the looking."

"That's great, Arnold. Let me tell you what I'm thinking. Suppose Iris got married because she was pregnant. She stays married long enough to make the baby legitimate and then decides she doesn't want to keep it—or keeping it would be too tough on her family. She gives the baby up, goes to Reno, and gets a divorce."

"Sounds plausible."

"Can we find out if she gave birth?"

"Not easy if we don't have a date. You have any idea how many babies are born every day in New York, even during the Depression?"

"I guess it's a lot."

"We don't know what hospital, what borough even. I'll do what I can, but it'll take time and I may not find anything. You have a birth date for this Iris Grodnik?"

"I do." I wrote it down for him.

"She born in this country?"

"In New York. She was the youngest. The oldest ones were born in Europe and came over as children."

"Sounds like my father's family. If we have to get out to check any records at the Board of Health, I'll have them look her up, too, but I can't promise."

"You feel something because your family was like her family."

"Can't help it. All our families shared the sorrows and joys of the twentieth century. There'll never be another one like it."

"This case, and the last one I worked on, have made me very aware of the pull of the family. You move across the country and you lose a lot of friends, but you never lose your family. For better or worse, they're all still there."

"Sounds like you're thinking of starting one of your own."

"I guess I am."

"Well, you're talking to the wrong man. Talk to that fine husband of yours. I'm sure he's on the same wavelength as you. I expect Harriet would set aside a little time in her busy life and knit you an heirloom if she got the news."

"Oh, Arnold, what a lovely thought."

"Lovely thought for a lovely person."

"Tell me why you think Iris's birth certificate is important."

"Everything's important. The cops probably didn't look it up because it's a trip out to Brooklyn and they don't feel like making it and they don't think it'll help. Maybe they're right, but it might yield something. You've got a person here who was probably killed by someone who knew her, someone she was going out to say hello to and instead he killed her. You've talked to the cops, her family, the people she worked with, and you've got nothing. Maybe there's something in her life that'll lead us to the killer. If you want to know all there is about a person, you don't look only at today. You look backward. Where did they start from to get here and now? Some of the nicest people I know have what you might call a past. Maybe she was adopted at birth, the child of a friend or relative of the people who raised her. There are lots of possibilities. You find any friends of hers?"

"She had a best friend named Shirley Finster." I told him what I had learned from the police file.

"Sounds like she didn't want a face-to-face interview. Maybe she knows something and doesn't want to tell."

"I don't know how to find her, Arnold. She could

be anywhere in the country and her last name could be anything."

"So we keep trying. How's the pasta?"

"Terrific."

"Just leave room for dessert. I won't have any if you don't, and I have a yen for something sweet."

"I'll join you." I glanced at the dessert menu with all its tantalizing offerings. "It's her boss I can't quite picture in all this."

"Garganus?"

"Yes. Why was he paying her if she wasn't working? Why did his wife know she was going to Europe and no one in the family knew? Is it possible he drove over or had his chauffeur drive him over to see Iris that night? Could a chauffeur have kept quiet about what he must have seen?"

"I think you're taking too many giant steps. Let's see what we can find out about the ex-husband."

"OK. And I'll have the cheesecake."

There were a slew of Handlemans in the metropolitan area, several of them *M*s and Martins. I made a list but didn't call any. Instead, I sat at my desk and did the work for my class so that I wouldn't have to think about it till next Tuesday. It's always nice to have that behind me.

Then I just sat back and thought. I tried to incorporate all the small details I had learned, that Marilyn's mother had spent so much time at Iris's apartment that her family had begun to worry about her, that Shirley Finster refused a face-to-face interview with the police, that Iris was unofficially working for GAR, but no one

knew what was going on. An ex-husband. A child ...
Maybe it was the child she had been supporting, although by the time she was murdered, the child would
have been in his late thirties.

I had no more answers when Jack came home than I
had had when he left in the morning, but I did have a
tentative theory. "Aunt Sylvie and Marilyn's mother
cleaned out Iris's apartment," I told him at the kitchen
table. "They're Iris's sister and sister-in-law. That was
sixteen years ago. Last weekend Marilyn's father became very angry when he heard we'd been in his apartment and had found Iris's handbag."

"Why not?" Jack said. "It's his place. Why should he
relinquish his privacy and authority just because he's
old?"

"I think it's more than that. I think there's something
in that apartment he doesn't want us to find, specifically
that he doesn't want Marilyn to find. I'm not a member
of the family, but she is."

"So the mother found papers in Iris's apartment and
took them home with her."

"Papers or something. And we'll never find out what
they are because he's going back to that apartment, and
when he gets there he'll destroy it."

"You're telling me he knows who killed his sister
and he's been hiding it from the police since her
death?"

"Maybe it's not who killed her but something about
her that he doesn't want the world to know. And maybe
he does know, or thinks he knows, and he's decided not
to say because it's Iris's own child."

"Aha."

"You know, you and Arnold sometimes respond the same way when I come up with an interesting idea."

"It's all those classes in law. Sometimes all you can think of saying is 'aha.' "

16

There's a point in every case when you feel you're at a standstill, and I woke up on Thursday morning convinced that I had reached it. I wanted to talk to Shirley Finster, but I had no idea how to find her. I wanted to find Martin Handleman, but it seemed a hopeless task unless Arnold located a marriage license and by some chance Mr. Handleman was still living where he had lived over fifty years ago, not very likely, especially since he and Iris had presumably moved into the apartment on the Grand Concourse together. And could there be a child, a problem child sent to live with another family, adopted perhaps or in a foster home? Such a child could understandably harbor tremendous resentment if his life turned out to be difficult, if he was unloved or perhaps the victim of an illness.

So it seemed that I had pushed my resources about as far as I could, including Mrs. Garganus, who I was sure knew much more than she had said. Why would Iris be planning a trip to Europe after pretending to quit her job? The answer might be quite simple, that in gratitude for years of overtime, Mr. Garganus had decided to give her a kind of sabbatical but didn't want it generally known since other people might expect or demand the same privilege. And if that was the answer to my question, it wasn't very helpful in explaining how and why Iris died.

I was about to call Sylvie and ask her a few questions when my phone rang. At the other end was my sister-in-law.

"Chris," Eileen said, "can we get together and talk?"

"Sure thing. Want to come up here or should I meet you in New York?"

"You do so much driving and it's so hard to park down here. Why don't I come up and leave my car in your driveway?"

"That's fine. Has anything happened with Taffy?"

"Something has and I want to talk to you about it before I talk to anyone else."

"What time?"

"Noonish. And I'll bring lunch. I want to try out something. I've been diddling with it for a while and I think it's coming together."

I smiled. "I'm sure it's great, Eileen. I'll see you in a couple of hours."

I was very glad she was coming. While I'm sure her parents and Jack were a great support for her, I've learned in my still new secular life that putting your head together with another woman is not only a comfort but can really be illuminating. What a wonderful discovery it was for me to find out that other women had gone through similar experiences to mine—and survived them—and that they had insights that could really help me make important decisions.

I made sure my kitchen was gleaming and picked up the living room. Then I called Sylvie.

"Chris?" she said in her little birdlike voice. "Chris from last Friday?"

"That's the one. How are you doing?"

"Oh, pretty good. You know, this hurts and that hurts, but I'm coming along. You finding out anything about Iris?"

"A few things. I wondered if you could help me a little more. I understand you and Marilyn's mother cleaned out Iris's apartment after she died."

"Oh, we did. What an awful job that was, seeing all those beautiful things my sister had that she would never use again, such clothes, and the dishes, and all the antiques."

"What happened to those things?" I asked.

"I got some, Abe got some, my other brother was alive then and he got some."

"What about the personal things, Sylvie? Iris must have had letters and address books, things like that." I almost had my fingers crossed.

"You're right. I remember the letters. She had a lot of them. I think my sister-in-law threw them away. What good are somebody else's letters? Iris was never going to read them again."

The matter-of-factness in her voice surprised me. She was so affected by her sister's death, it seemed out of character for her to talk about a very personal possession that way. "Did you find an address book?"

"I guess we must have. I think we threw all that stuff away."

Or left it at Abraham Grodnik's apartment, I thought. "Do you know if Iris kept up with her former husband?"

"Kept up with him? You mean if they talked to each other?"

"Yes."

"I don't think so. I don't think they got along at all. When it was over, he moved out and that was the end. That's what I remember."

"Did he support her at all?"

"You mean like alimony? I don't think Iris would take it from him. She was very young when she married him. My parents didn't like him at all. I don't think they would have let Iris take money from him."

An age when parents could tell their daughters what to do and what not to do and the daughters would listen—except that Iris had married against their will. "Do you have any idea how I can get in touch with Shirley Finster?"

"Oh, Shirley. I haven't seen her in years."

"Did you see her after Iris died?"

"I'm sure she came to the funeral. Maybe I ran into her after that. I'm not sure."

"Is she married, Sylvie?"

"Shirley Finster? I think maybe she is."

"Do you know what her name is now or where she lives?"

"You should ask Abe. Abe will know."

"Sylvie, when we were talking last Friday you said you know something no one else would tell me. Would you tell me what that is?"

"Well." She was quiet for a moment. "Maybe I was thinking of Iris's marriage. My brother wouldn't tell you that. But you knew about it, right?"

"Yes, I heard. Harry Schiff told me."

"Harry! You found Harry?"

"Yes. He's a very nice man."

"He's the one Iris should've married. She'd still be alive if she married him."

"Why do you say that?"

"Harry would have taken care of her. He was a good man."

Last Friday she had told me Harry was her sister's killer.

If Abraham Grodnik was the man I thought he was, he would not relent. If he had kept his secrets sixteen years after the death of his sister, he wasn't likely to give them up now. What he would do, I was quite certain, was return to his apartment and destroy any documents that might indicate that Iris had had a husband or a child, and there was nothing we could do about it. Sylvie had not convinced me that the secret she had thought of telling me was Iris's marriage. She had sounded hesitant, as though it was convenient to use the marriage as her secret, thus giving herself an out. I didn't like it. If Iris had had a child, Sylvie might well have known and might be persuaded to talk about it if I could think of a way to get her to open up. But I didn't know how.

So it appeared that I was faced with several implacable people, Abraham, Sylvie, and Mrs. Garganus. And that meant that it was time for me to call in my secret weapon.

Sister Joseph is the General Superior of St. Stephen's Convent. I met her the night I entered the convent as a frightened fifteen-year-old and we grew to become close friends. She is older than I and is serving her first term as Superior, having been elected before I left. She is a wonderful mix of the traditional and the modern, with a mind that reaches out to both, and she has marvelously perceptive insights that have helped me in my personal life and also in my investigations. This morning I knew I had to tap that resource.

Sister Angela answered the phone and bubbled with excitement when she heard my voice. "Chris, it's wonderful to hear from you. How are you and Jack?"

"We're doing fine. Jack's started talking about adding onto the house, and I'm a little nervous."

"You worry too much. He's probably a better judge than you when it comes to that kind of thing."

"I thought you'd be on my side. Everyone up there takes Jack's side."

"Well, you managed to marry a wonderful man. What can I say? Hold on. I've got a call coming in." She left my line and came back a minute later. "Hello again. I bet you want Joseph."

"If she's available."

"She is and you've got her."

The next voice was Joseph's. "Chris, how do you always manage to call when I'm thinking of you?"

"I guess we're on the same wavelength. I only call when I'm thinking of you, too."

She laughed. "Are we getting a visit? And maybe something to tickle a mind in need of some extra activity?"

"Both if you'll have me."

"Wonderful. Let me look at my schedule." A page turned. "For a change I seem to have a clear week. Pick your day."

"How's tomorrow?"

"Aha, it must be a tough puzzle. Tomorrow's fine. Come early and stay for lunch."

"I will." Aha indeed.

17

Eileen turned up the driveway just before twelve and we hugged in the living room as she entered, holding her packages aloft to protect them. We laughed and I was relieved to see that she looked like her usual self, her face pretty and her hair a modified version of Jack's unruly curls.

"I'm glad to be here," she said, heading right for the kitchen with her offerings. "If Mom calls me one more time to see how I am, I may tell her the truth."

"Well, you're looking good. Do we eat first?"

"We heat first, then eat and talk at the same time, the way I've done it all my life."

"Let me turn on the oven."

"Oh, Chris, I forgot. You haven't entered the twentieth century yet, have you? Still no microwave?"

"Still no microwave. Jack had one in his Brooklyn Heights apartment, and I thought it was wonderful. Even St. Stephen's got one recently. But I haven't changed the house very much from the way Aunt Meg left it." I turned the oven on and looked inside the big bag. "Home-baked rolls?"

"Sourdough. Put them in the oven. They're better

warm. The chicken salad should be just right, and when the rolls come out, we can put the dessert in."

"One of your super treats, I bet."

"Cherry cobbler. Old-fashioned and always good. Well, you look exactly like yourself, and that's the best thing anyone can say about you."

"So do you." I took dishes out and set the table. "Coffee?"

"Oh yes. My brother and I can't live without it."

I got it going and Eileen checked the rolls. Then she dished up a beautiful chicken salad.

"It smells heavenly. What did you put in it?"

"Curry. I love it this way. And I've added a few other Indian spices. I need your honest opinion."

"Eileen, you know I love everything you make."

She took the rolls out and put them on the bread plates, then put the cobbler in the oven. "Just be honest. I'm always afraid I'll overdo some favorite spice of mine because I love it so much. You have to tell me if it's too strong. Sometimes I have to work very hard to balance the subtlety with my personal taste."

I sat down and took a forkful of the salad. "It's wonderful. Don't change a thing."

"Just keep eating. Let me know at the end if it's still as appealing as the first bite was."

"I'm so glad I have you and Jack in the family. It really eases my conscience that I'm an awful cook."

"You aren't awful at all. You have simple tastes and you make simple food. There's nothing wrong with that."

"You know, I picked Jack, but I really lucked out on his family."

"So did we. I want to talk about Taffy."

"Go on."

"Jack told you what happened."

"Yes."

"Here goes. This is very painful, Chris. I've known Taffy all my life and we're like sisters. We've worked together since day one, and even though we haven't agreed on everything, we've done better than most partners. When Taffy wrote that check and disappeared, I felt—" She stopped and swallowed. "Devastated." Her eyes filled. "If Jack cleaned out your bank account and left you, you'd feel the way I felt. Abandoned. Betrayed. I couldn't believe it. It was not only self-serving, it destroyed me as well."

"I understand."

"I felt sore inside, as though I'd drunk some cleaning fluid and it left all my organs raw. As much as I had loved her, that's how much I hate her now." She looked at my dish. "Your last bite. Tell me, are the spices too strong? Has the impact worn off?"

I smiled. In the midst of her tears, she was a professional. "It's terrific, Eileen. If my life ever permits me to entertain a group of women, I'll order this chicken salad for the main course."

"Thanks, Chris." She took another bite, savoring it. "I'm glad you agree. I really didn't want to make it more delicate. Anyway. I got a letter from Taffy yesterday and I've been stewing about it. I can't talk to Mom and Dad about it because they're another generation, and as broad-minded as they usually are, this is something that I think is beyond their ability to cope with. The truth is, I don't know exactly how you'll react, so I'm going to talk to you in a kind of general way. OK?"

"Sure." I got up and took the dessert out of the oven,

put it on plates, and poured coffee. The cherries smelled better than anything I had cooked since Christmas (with Melanie's help), and my mouth was watering when I sat down.

"She took the money to help someone."

"OK."

"It was someone close to her, her sister." She said this almost reluctantly, as though she wanted to keep identities hidden.

"A sister's about as close as you can get. If you don't help your sister, I don't know who you do help."

"That's the way I feel. And if it's your sister, you don't sit down with her and say, 'I know you have a problem, but you got yourself into this mess and you should get yourself out of it.' You help her."

"Because if you don't help her, the situation will get worse."

"Much worse. And there's time later to let her know she should run her life so she doesn't get into this kind of trouble."

"Right. After you've gotten her out of the difficulty she's in."

"I'm glad you're following. So this is what happened. When Taffy's sister came to her with her problem, Taffy panicked. Her sister needed the money right away, Taffy didn't have it, neither one of them could borrow it, and Taffy did the only thing she knew to do."

"She wrote a check from the catering account."

"And decided to deal with the consequences later."

"It's a lot of money, Eileen."

"It's not only a lot of money, it was all the money we had."

"And you needed at least some of it to keep your business going."

"Yes. And she knew it. She knew our business as well as I did."

"I have one question that's bothering me," I said. "Jack said that Taffy was planning a trip, and when she left, she was presumably going on that trip."

"That's right."

"Did she know about her sister's problem at the time she booked the vacation?"

"I don't think so. I think she truly intended to take a vacation and then this thing happened and she just worked it out so that she withdrew the money when I expected her to leave, so I wasn't surprised that she wasn't there and I didn't know the money was gone for several days."

"It was kind of a fortuitous coincidence."

"Yes, right." Eileen sipped her coffee.

"Has Taffy's sister's problem been taken care of?"

"She wrote that it had. Yes, I think that's out of the way for good now." She fiddled with her cobbler, which was delicious, and sipped more coffee.

I sensed where she was going, but I didn't want to put words into her mouth. And I didn't want to tell her how much I enjoyed her lunch for fear of getting her off a track she wasn't very comfortable riding. "OK," I said noncommittally.

"Well, here's the thing. Taffy feels—Taffy wants—" She began to choke up again, the enormity of her love and affection for her lifelong friend overcoming her. "Taffy wants me to forgive her." The tears spilled over and she pulled a tissue out of her pocket and put her head in her hands.

"I know how much you love her, Eileen. I have some friends I feel the same way about."

"I'm just so—I'm torn into little pieces over this. I want so much for us to be friends again, to sit and giggle together like we did when we were little. I just don't know if we can."

"But that's different," I said.

"I don't follow you."

"You said Taffy wanted you to forgive her."

"She does."

"I think you already have. I think your feelings for her are so deep that as soon as you knew she was doing something to save her sister, you forgave her. But you may not have excused her behavior, and you may want to think about whether you really want to do that."

"I see what you mean."

"Taffy did some things that you may feel are inexcusable. She stole money from you."

"I hate to use that word."

"I know you do. That's why I used it. Half of it was probably hers."

"It was."

"But she didn't have a right to take even her share without discussing it with you first."

"That's part of our agreement."

"I'm sure that if she had come to you and told you the situation her sister was in, you would have tried to work out some kind of accommodation."

"Oh, Chris, I would. I would have done anything. If I'd gone to a bank with our record and all our money in the checking account, I could have borrowed more."

"But she didn't and so you couldn't."

"I know."

"And she left you in a terrible position. Of course you want to forgive her. You don't want Taffy to spend the rest of her life with this awful thing hanging over her head, knowing she hurt you and you're incapable of forgiving her. But forgiving doesn't mean that you pick up where you left off. Both of your lives have changed. You can't ignore that."

"They're two separate things, aren't they?"

"I think they are."

"Then if I write her back—I think that's easier than calling—and tell her she's forgiven, I have to make it clear that our partnership and our giggling together don't come along for the ride."

It's a funny thing about giving advice. A piece of the burden slips from the asker's shoulders to the giver's, and as I sat there, I was conscious of the weight of Eileen's decision, an uncomfortable weight. I had met Taffy only briefly at our wedding, which their company had catered, but I felt for her, felt the pain of her being asked by her sister for help, the additional pain of taking something that wasn't hers because there was no one else and the sister needed the money because she had done something wrong or stupid. But my main concern was for Eileen. Not only had she been effectively bankrupted by her friend's action, she had suffered emotionally, and was still suffering.

"You know I can't tell you what to do."

"I'm not asking you to. I just want to hear how you feel, and what you've said so far is really very helpful."

"Did she say anything about repaying the money?"

"She said her sister will make good, but it's going to be a long time. Personally, I'm not sure we'll ever get it all back."

"You sound like a realist, Eileen."

"I'm in business. I've learned a lot in the last few years, a lot of it things I wish I'd never had to learn. This is probably the worst."

"It's probably the worst for your whole life. Maybe that's how you should look at it. After this, everything's going to be easier."

She tried to smile. "You think I shouldn't give Taffy a second chance."

"I think this is the hardest decision you'll ever have to make and you shouldn't make it too quickly. Some time has to pass. The business part of you has to talk to the part of you that's a friend."

"Because they're in conflict."

"I think they are."

"I wish we could just go back a month and do this over the right way."

"Let's go for a walk."

"Good idea."

We got our coats and went outside. It was a bright, cool, spring day. We were only weeks away from that wonderful period when the trees leafed out, the tulips and daffodils bloomed, the pink and purple trees showed their color for a brief time before the green leaves took over for the rest of the season. I couldn't wait.

"I always thought Jack was a city person," Eileen said, looking around Pine Brook Road with its quiet houses. "I couldn't imagine him ever living in a place like this, and he loves it."

"I'm glad. I'm not a city person, and when I come back from New York and get off the parkway and onto the little roads, I feel a sense of relief. And it smells so good here."

"It does, doesn't it?"

We walked by Mel's house and I thought of Iris for a moment. "Were you surprised when Taffy asked you to put it all behind?"

"Very. I thought she was gone for good. I thought I'd never see or hear from her for the rest of my life. I was resigned to it. It made it easier for me to hate her."

"In a convent close friendships are frowned upon."

"But you're close to Sister Joseph."

"Yes. But we never giggled together."

"Does that make you sad?"

"I've never thought about it. I had wonderful years at St. Stephen's. If there are things that I missed, there are also things I experienced that most other people haven't. I've never made a list of pluses and minuses or assets and liabilities, and I don't intend to."

"Taffy was always there for me. Once, when a boy-friend ditched me, I don't think I could have gotten through it without her."

"That's one of the experiences I missed in my life."

"Don't cry over it," Eileen said, laughing. "I think it took ten years off my life."

"I expect it added to it. It made you smarter. And maybe tougher."

"Not smart enough," she said.

"You'll do the right thing, Eileen."

"It just hurts so damn much."

18

I called a lot of Handlemans in the evening and got nowhere. There were Martins who were too young, Martins who had died and whose wives had retained their names in the phone book, and a lot of responses that convinced me they didn't know what I was talking about. I don't think I ever found any Martin Handleman seventy-five or older, so it was all a dead end.

I told Jack about Eileen's visit and added that I had given her a check for two thousand dollars before she left. Since I married Jack, my inheritance has gone unused. I'm not a very aggressive investor and I've tended to leave Aunt Meg's money the way she had it, mostly government notes and a few stocks I've heard called "widow and orphan" investments. All I know is that checks come in from time to time, and when they accumulate, I do something with the money that will earn it more interest. Jack thinks we'll be millionaires someday, but I suspect we'll call on those funds to build a family room or put a child through school. Or both. It isn't anything I worry about. But Eileen told me I now had an "interest" in her business, whatever that means, and she suggested I was now a venture capitalist. Whatever *that* means!

On Friday morning I dressed more formally than my usual jeans since I like to look acceptable when I visit the nuns. When Jack left for Brooklyn, I got in my car and drove west to the Hudson River and north to St. Stephen's, a trip my car knows so well I sometimes think the turn signals go on before I touch them.

I had a lot to think about as I drove. The lunch with Eileen had added to my growing perceptions about family. The elder Grodniks had kept secrets from their children; Eileen would not discuss Taffy's problems with her parents. The reasons were different. The Grodniks were embarrassed about certain things like divorce; Eileen felt her mother would not understand because she was the "older" generation. But the outcome was the same. The indiscretions of a generation stayed there.

I had little doubt what Taffy's sister's indiscretion had been, and I was slightly amused at Eileen's decision not to tell me, although she must surely have known I had guessed. I suppose that coming from a convent, I inspire certain expectations in people, expectations that may be far from accurate. While I don't discuss the intimate details of my life with other people, except perhaps in confession, I had what is generally called an affair with Jack before we were married. I think I surprised myself when I did it, but I never felt guilty. I felt conflicted because it forced me into small lies when I spoke to people like Joseph and it kept me from mass until I found a wonderful priest with whom I could talk. Happily, there are such people and I was able to set my conflict aside. That Jack felt none of my concerns has never troubled me.

But as I drove up the Hudson on the old road, I

thought about Taffy's sister and Iris Grodnik and how families come together to protect their own.

As usual, my heart skipped a beat at the first sight of the tallest spire of St. Stephen's and my vital functions quickened at the approach of the convent. It is a beautiful place. A private road winds from the entrance to the Mother House, where I left my car in the nearby lot. Beyond that there are paths and lanes to the various buildings, across fields and through trees that on this morning had not yet leafed out. After I parked I treated myself to a solitary walk and the sense of renewal that always accompanies it.

I ran into no brown-habited Franciscan nuns and passed only a few students, none of whom I knew. St. Stephen's College, where I taught for many years, is beyond the original buildings of the convent and I stayed away from it, preferring to pass the Villa, where the retired nuns live, and the chapel where Jack and I were married.

When my body felt loosened by my walk, I returned to the chapel and stepped inside. Two nuns knelt in prayer near the front, one on the left, one on the right, neither aware of the other's presence or of mine. I fetched three candles, left an equal number of dollars for them, and lit one each for my mother, my father, and my aunt Meg, an old practice of mine when I enter a church. I hope to go to Rome someday and light them at St. Peter's.

Then I sat in a rear pew, not praying, just enjoying the peace of the place and the moment. This chapel is left open twenty-four hours a day, and at night it isn't uncommon to find one or two sleepless nuns sitting or kneeling in a pew, often the older ones from the Villa.

Many times when I was a nun I walked inside for morning prayers to find a nun who had surely spent much of the night there. But what I thought of that Friday morning was the day last August when Jack and I were married here. The sun was so bright that the windows were ablaze. There were flowers and white ribbons and the beautiful altar linens Jack's mother had given the convent as a gift and which had been handmade by one of the nuns with a talent for embroidery and a joy in her work.

One of the nuns let out a sigh or a moan, and I stood and eased myself out of the pew, not wanting to disturb or break the silence. Outside, I turned left and walked along the path Jack and I had taken as husband and wife back to the Mother House.

"There you are, Kix," a familiar voice called as I stepped inside. It was Angela, who was usually on bells in the small telephone room not far from the entrance. "You look great. How was the drive?"

I hugged her. "Easy as pie. That car of mine turns corners before I know I'm there."

"Are you staying for lunch?"

"Absolutely."

"Maybe I'll see you then. Unless you and Joseph have a long tête-à-tête upstairs."

"It's hard to tell. I'm working on an old murder and I need a clear head and some direction."

"You came to the right place. Go on up. I'll ring her you're coming."

The Mother House is built like a fortress. It's old and made of stone, and something in me loves to walk up those wide, worn steps to the second floor. Joseph's office is at the far end of the hall, giving her a corner and windows on two sides. She opened the door before I knocked, and we hugged and exchanged greetings as we walked inside.

"The carafe is full," she said as we separated to sit on opposite sides of the long conference table, our usual seating arrangement when I came up for assistance. "And Sister Dolores came and baked muffins this morning when she heard you were coming."

Dolores had been in charge of the Christmas dinner Jack and I had shared with the convent a few months earlier. She was one of the nuns in the Villa, a woman in her seventies who refused to consider herself either old or unable to contribute. "That sounds wonderful. I should probably take cooking lessons from her. I still leave the exotic cooking to Jack."

"And your wonderful neighbor."

"And to Melanie. It's still a wonder to me that she made Christmas cookies in my kitchen for the first time in her life and they were perfect."

"Well, you have other fine attributes. You've been outdoing the police for some time now."

"This one is a toughie, Joseph," I said as she passed the basket of still warm muffins to me.

"Good. Those are the ones I like best."

"It's Melanie's great-aunt," I began, "a woman named Iris Grodnik who was murdered in New York about sixteen years ago. And it happened while the family was celebrating Passover."

"Then you're probably learning while you work."

"I certainly am. Toward the end of the seder a cup of wine is poured for the prophet Elijah and someone opens the door to the house or apartment so he can get in. In this case, the woman who opened the door put her coat on, left her pocketbook behind, and went outside. Two days later her body was found in an oil yard at the northern tip of Manhattan, several miles away."

Joseph reached for the pile of white, unlined paper that she kept at the end of the table and uncapped a pen. "She went to meet her killer," she said.

"Perhaps." And then I told her the story.

There is something about retelling that is in itself useful. It forces you to recall details, to put them in context, to organize events and discoveries. But beyond that, when you relate information to a perceptive listener, you are asked questions that must be answered or investigated further, and the listener's point of view often brings to light other areas that should be looked into and makes you consider possibilities you never thought of.

Joseph didn't bombard me with questions, but she asked several. "Why the oil yards?" was one.

I shrugged. "He had a body. He had to do something with it. Why not the oil yards?"

"Not an acceptable response," she said. "If I had committed a murder in Manhattan and had to get rid of a body, I'd probably try to dump it in one of the parks, Central Park or Riverside Park. They're large and accessible; you can drive there day or night."

"Maybe he knew the northern part of Manhattan. Maybe he'd lived there. An awful lot of people do."

"Go on, go on. Don't let me get you off course."

I told her everything I knew and everywhere I'd gone, referring to my notes and forgetting nothing. I mentioned my visit to GAR and my subsequent visit to Mrs. Garganus and her granddaughter, the unexplained facts of Iris's departure from the company. I told her about our visit to Abraham Grodnik's apartment, the discovery of the handbag, and Mr. Grodnik's reaction when he heard Marilyn and I had been there. I described my talk with Detective Harris White and my meeting with Harry Schiff, Iris's old boyfriend. And I talked about my meeting and phone conversation with Aunt Sylvie and my uneasiness about her secret.

"From the beginning," I said finally, "Iris's family, that is, Marilyn Margulies mostly, but I think she speaks for the family, has felt that Iris went outside that night of the seder to meet someone she knew and give him something, perhaps money that a friend or a co-worker needed to borrow. Everyone says Iris was a good friend, a person who would help you if you were in need. But if it was a co-worker—and that seems increasingly unlikely—I don't know how to find her, and some of them are no longer living. Most of her family was present at the seder, so it couldn't have been any of them. That doesn't leave many possibilities."

Joseph looked thoughtful for a moment. "Let me just review what's missing. You know nothing about the ex-husband."

"That's right. Aunt Sylvie told me approximately when they were married and that it was a bad marriage. It didn't last a year. And none of the Handlemans I called last night seemed right for the part."

"And you haven't been able to find the best friend."

"Not a clue. Shirley Finster. Aunt Sylvie thinks she may have married, but she doesn't know the new name. I think there must be an address book—or was an address book—that belonged to Iris. If it exists, it's in Mr. Grodnik's apartment, and he will never let us see it."

"Because there's something he doesn't want you to

know about Iris. That's really what we have to think about."

"I think she could have had a child," I said. "One of my theories is that she married to legitimize a child or she became pregnant while she was married."

"But the child isn't part of the family."

"She would have given it up. In a family where divorce was considered anathema, imagine what they would think of an illegitimate child."

"Or a legitimate one that the mother gave up because she felt she couldn't raise it herself. Can you find out if such a child was born to her?"

"It's very difficult, Joseph. Arnold Gold will do his best, but he really needs a date, and a location would help a lot."

She smiled at the mention of Arnold. They had met at our wedding and discovered they had much to talk about. "And if the child was given up for adoption, the records are probably sealed and we have no idea what the child's name would be. I hope that's not the answer because it sounds like a dead end. Let me leave that for a moment. I'm interested in your perception that Mrs. Garganus knows more than she's willing to tell you."

"We had a very brief conversation that lasted only until she got me to the front door, and it started with her saying she knew nothing about Iris except that she was the best secretary her husband had ever had and in the next sentence she was suggesting that Iris was taking an extended vacation to Europe, specifically to Switzerland. For a woman who knew nothing about Iris, she certainly knew a lot more than Iris's family did."

"They had no inkling she was going to travel?"

"They didn't know she'd quit her job."

"So something is indeed very strange there. Could you manage to see her again?"

"Not if she sees me first."

"Did you have the feeling her granddaughter was visiting or that she lived there?"

"She must be living there. Mrs. Garganus said she'd stayed home from school because she had a cold. If she was going to school in that area, she must live there. And she had a room she went up to."

"I wonder if she knows anything."

"She couldn't. She's a teenager, fifteen or sixteen years old. I'm a terrible judge of age, especially adolescents."

"Do you know her name, Chris?"

"Erin Garganus. She told me. She must be the Garganuses' son's child. Maybe the parents are divorced."

"Maybe," Joseph said thoughtfully. "You should check that. This is very interesting. Yes, very interesting indeed."

"I'm not sure I see where you're going."

"I'm not entirely sure myself. She must be about the age you were when you came to St. Stephen's."

"Chronologically, I suppose so, but we're as different as two teenagers could be. She's packed with self-confidence."

"A tribute to her grandmother, no doubt. I wonder sometimes how today's children manage to reach adulthood whole; they have so many problems to overcome that aren't of their making. Of course, you managed."

"With a little help."

"Yes." She smiled. "And the oil yards. I keep coming

back to them. There are vacant lots all over Manhattan, two large parks, many small ones, heaps of garbage lining the streets at night waiting to be collected, and a deep river a few blocks east or west of any point on the island. Why does he drive to the farthest point in Manhattan when so many accessible places are closer?"

I had no answer. "Maybe Jack and I can drive down there tomorrow."

"Poor Jack," Joseph said. "Two days off every week and he spends one of them visiting the scene of a crime."

"I'll tell him you were concerned. Without him and Arnold, I'd never get anywhere. And you," I added. "You always seem to know."

"I don't know anything, but I have healthy suspicions. And here's one of them. Everyone seems so certain that Iris went outside that fateful night to give something to someone, presumably something she had in her coat pocket since her handbag was left behind. But suppose you're all wrong. Suppose she went downstairs to meet someone who was giving her something."

She was right; it was a possibility I had never entertained. "But what could it have been? Nothing was found on her body except her clothes."

"And that may be the real mystery. Iris went down without her purse because she was expecting something small enough to fit in her coat pocket or hold in her hand till she went back upstairs. Did the man she met have second thoughts and refuse to give her the thing she expected? Did he give it and take it back, prompting a fight to the death? Was it the wrong thing or too little of the right thing? Or did something else happen that we cannot even imagine at this moment?"

19

Friday is the day my husband comes home for dinner. There are no evening classes, and unless he gets caught up in a case, which happens occasionally, he's home at a reasonable hour and we have a weekend to look forward to. It's also a night that Jack isn't dog-tired, which adds to the happy mixture.

On that Friday he was home by seven and we had our arms around each other as he stepped inside the house.

"Mm, must have been an inspiring trip," he said, kissing me for the second time.

"It was. It's good to see you before the moon comes out."

"And I turn into a sleepwalker. Anything cooking?"

"Not yet. Salmon steaks ready to go."

"Could they wait?"

"I think so. You feeling single and sexy?"

"Well, not single, but we could maybe go upstairs."

"Maybe."

"Definitely."

We went.

I was feeling rosy and happy when I came back down and turned on the broiler. The salad was ready and I would let Jack mix his favorite dressing and do the honors with the salmon. I cut up a grapefruit while he changed his clothes, and when he came down, he got to work on the dressing.

"Sister Joseph solve it for you?"

"Not quite, but as usual, she's full of ideas. One of her big ones is the oil yards. Why did he dump the body up there when there are so many other places in Manhattan he could have used?"

"Let's look at a map after we eat."

"The other thing is, she thinks Iris may have gone downstairs to meet someone who was giving *her* something, not the other way around."

"Interesting."

"And that some misunderstanding erupted into a fight that led to her murder."

"She have any idea what was given?"

"If she did, she didn't tell me." I put the grapefruit halves on the table as he finished the dressing and turned the salmon. "OK?"

"Yup." He sat and we started eating. "You have any idea yet who this mysterious gift giver is?"

"I keep thinking Mr. Garganus even though I never liked the idea that he was the killer. But his house is so close to the Grodniks' apartment he could have walked there easily."

"That means Iris was in contact with him. She told him she was going to be there and approximately what time she could come downstairs to see him."

"So they had some kind of relationship outside of the job."

"Maybe it was a payoff," Jack said. "He gives her

some money, maybe a lot of money, and kisses her good-bye."

"Then why was she still on the payroll?"

"Good question."

"But assuming he did give her some money that night, maybe someone saw the exchange, and when Garganus left, this stranger came over and robbed her."

"A crime of opportunity by a guy who just happened to have a car nearby so he could take her up to the oil yards and kill her?"

"A little hard to believe," I admitted.

"But," my husband said with a grin, "hard-to-believe things have been known to happen. Who knows? It could have been a crime of opportunity after all, someone getting out of his car at just the right moment. Or, going back to the old idea that she gave her killer something, maybe you're right that Iris had had a child, and maybe that child caused her all kinds of trouble that she couldn't afford to keep paying for. She goes downstairs with a bunch of bills in her pocket, meets the son, says this is the last payment ever, kid, and he takes it and kills her."

"I hate to think about a child killing his mother."

"You hate to think about anyone killing anyone, but it happens, it happens in families, and somebody killed Iris."

"If it was Garganus, why would he give her money?" I said to myself.

"In payment for years of work well done, maybe more than that. Iris had decided to take some time off, enjoy life, have a good time. Maybe with *M*, who she's seeing tomorrow. Remember *M*? Garganus gives her cash, of course, because he doesn't want the company to know or even his wife. Cash, if you remember, is highly negotiable. Somebody's watching, sees the exchange, takes the money, kills Iris, and disposes of her body."

"So there could have been a killer besides Mr. Garganus. Does he see what happens? Does he see the killer with Iris? Does he see her get into the killer's car?"

"Maybe he does and maybe he doesn't. It's not unheard-of for witnesses to fail to come forward. His wife doesn't know where he is that night, thinks he's just gone out for his late evening walk, maybe walking the dog. If she finds out he's involved with Iris—who turns up dead two days later, remember—there'll be hell to pay at home."

"So he keeps quiet and dies ten or twelve years later, never having told the secret."

"It happens. Good salmon. We haven't had it for a while."

"Quick and easy. And good for you."

"You're good for me."

"Not as good as salmon."

"You don't like my scenario."

"I don't dislike it, Jack. It's got some major problems. If it was a crime of opportunity, that's random and I'm back at square one. If it was her son, I can't find out if Iris ever had a child because her brother won't tell me."

"What about Aunt Sylvie?"

"I'll try, but I'm afraid she closed up last time I talked to her. I don't know if she'll open up again."

"Anything else?"

"Mr. Garganus. It doesn't fit. Mrs. Garganus knows

something. Why didn't she just tell me that her husband walked over there that night, gave Iris a bonus, and never saw Iris or the money again?"

"Assuming she knows, she's protecting his memory. He saw something he should have reported, but he kept it to himself. Even though he's dead, she doesn't want to admit her husband wasn't forthcoming."

"She doesn't have to tell me he saw anything. All she has to say is he took a walk, he gave her money, he never saw her again."

"Maybe she doesn't know he gave Iris money and maybe it wasn't money he gave her. Maybe it was a piece of jewelry," Jack said, scooping up the last of the salad.

"Glittering diamonds that he wanted back or someone else saw and killed her for? No. You don't hand out diamonds on a street corner."

"OK. You shoot that one down, I'll give you another. Maybe the gift had no intrinsic value. Maybe he handed her the key to the love nest you mentioned the other day."

"Mm. So they were consummating a relationship. But a key doesn't come with an address, and no one would kill her for a key except maybe Mr. Garganus to get it back."

"So you've got me. I'll tell you what he met her for. He hadn't seen her in days and he was aching for her. She was going to be at a seder a couple of blocks from his house, so they agreed to meet for one precious stolen moment. I think all he gave her was a kiss."

They say cops have no imagination, that they work by the book and find it hard to accept change. Maybe it's true for some or even most of them, but my husband has one terrific imagination. He isn't old enough to have seen everything, so I know it's more than experience, but he really comes up with ideas that are beyond anything I can think of. And I've read a lot more than he has.

There was something so touchingly sweet about Iris and her lover meeting for a kiss that I found myself accepting it just on Jack's offhand remark. It gave me a new scenario to think about: Garganus was indeed having an affair with Iris, and he did, in fact, talk to his wife about her, but only to tell her that Iris had quit her job and was planning a trip to Switzerland. Ergo, the wife no longer has anything to worry about. When she calls her husband at work, a new voice will answer, and when she drops into the office or comes to the next Christmas party, she will see a new face, perhaps one not quite so attractive as Iris's. And that would explain Wilfred Garganus's meeting with Iris the night of Passover, if, indeed, he met her.

But it didn't give me a killer. After the dishes were done, Jack hauled out some of his maps. I seem to find myself among map collectors. Aunt Meg saved every one of them that ever crossed her hand, and one of them helped me find a town in central New York State that no longer exists. Jack keeps current maps partly because he feels he should know every nook and cranny in the five boroughs, and now in Westchester as well.

"You see how the Bronx almost encloses Manhattan?" he said, pointing out the northern end of Manhattan and the western side of the Bronx. "The Bronx is the mainland, Manhattan is the island, and the Harlem River separates them. North of Manhattan, the Bronx juts out toward the west so that the west coastline of Manhattan runs right into the west coastline of the Bronx, with just the Spuyten Duyvil River between them. In effect, when the Harlem River turns west, it becomes the Spuyten Duyvil. It's the same body of water."

"This must be where the oil yards are," I said, touching the right side of the top of Manhattan.

"Right next to the subway yards. Ever wonder where subway trains sleep at night?"

"Never. But I guess that's the place."

"You could dump a body there, too," Jack said matter-of-factly. "But you'd have to be careful not to get it on a track or it'd be found in less than eight hours when the shift changes. OK, let's see what's in the neighborhood. You know about Baker Field."

"The Columbia football stadium. Marilyn told me about it."

"So maybe there's a Columbia connection." He had his folded piece of paper that he had started notes on the other day. Now he folded it to a clean side and wrote "Columbia" on it. "OK, here's Broadway, and this red line is the IRT subway. It's aboveground at that point and goes across the Spuyten Duyvil just north of the oil yards and ends up at Two Hundred Forty-second Street. That's the end of the line."

"I remember seeing the el when I went to the precinct."

"Broadway crosses the Spuyten Duyvil right here, just beyond the oil yards. Then you're in the Bronx, what's called the West Bronx. To get to the East Bronx by car, you just make a right turn at Two Hundred Twenty-fifth Street and that becomes Kingsbridge Road and goes across Jerome Avenue and then the Concourse."

"The Concourse," I said, finally recognizing a name. "The Grand Concourse?"

"That's the one."

"That looks like a very short drive."

"Five or ten minutes. Not far at all."

"Sylvie lives on the Grand Concourse right near Kingsbridge Road. We were there, Jack."

"So that's another connection." He wrote it down.

"This is scary. Someone in Sylvie's family. I can't believe it."

"She have a husband?"

"She did. I don't know when he died. But she's in her eighties. Sixteen years ago he would have been in his sixties or seventies."

"They have kids?"

"A son and a daughter took her away from the table when she started to cry at the seder."

"So if the son's sixty now, he could have been in his forties when Iris was killed."

"There's no motive, Jack."

"You just haven't found one."

"There's another connection to the Grand Concourse, though. When Iris was married, they lived on the Concourse."

"OK. And the husband may have stayed on. He could have driven across Two Hundred Twenty-fifth Street to Broadway, crossed the bridge into Manhattan, and picked up the Harlem River Drive right here."

"That would take him into the East Seventies."

"There's an exit in the Seventies. It's an easy drive."

"How does he know about the oil yards?"

"Maybe he went to Columbia and he wandered around the area before or after a football game. Maybe he uses a garage up there to service his car. Maybe he's been on a train and looked out the window. Remember, it's aboveground there."

"And maybe he lives in or grew up in the Inwood section at the northern end of Manhattan."

"All good possibilities."

"Could we go down and look at that oil yard, Jack? Like maybe tomorrow?"

"Ah, sweetheart, a Saturday without a visit to an oil yard is a lost day. Let's do it."

So we drove down there Saturday morning, passing Baker Field just before Jack turned, and a few seconds later we found ourselves as far from a city as one could be. There was the chain-link fence Marilyn had described, the oil tanks, the weeds, and the litter.

"No one could walk here at night," I said.

"You'd have to be crazy to want to."

Jack pointed out where the chain-link fence was less than secure; a hard pull in the right place would lift it out of the ground far enough for a person to crawl under. There were also a couple of useless, abandoned cabs of oil trucks rusting away, one with the door closed, the other with it hanging open, half off its hinges.

"Take a little longer to find her if you stuck her body in one of those," he said matter-of-factly.

"I don't think that's what the killer did. She was found pretty quickly."

We got out of the car. It was a sad-looking place, industrial, commercial, ugly, uninviting.

"Over that way," Jack said, pointing, "right across the Harlem River, is the Bronx. That's the Morris Heights section right there along the river. Then up this way the river is called the Spuyten Duyvil."

"Sounds Dutch."

"It is. They settled New York and left some of their names. Nice view."

"If you look in the right direction."

A loose dog was watching us from inside the fence. When we started to move, he started to bark. Where was he, I wondered, the night someone dumped the body of a little woman sixteen years ago?

"Let's look in on the security guard."

We walked to the shack near the truck entrance. This was where the oil trucks would leave with their cargo and return empty for a refilling. The guard saw us as we approached and opened his door. I could feel the heat of his little room pour out.

"Help you?" he said.

"We've got a couple of questions about an old homicide," Jack said. "Got a minute?"

"Sure. Come on in. I could use the company."

We went inside and sat on uncomfortable chairs that would keep anyone from staying very long. The guard sat on his chair, which looked like a much better bet.

"I'm Jack Brooks. This is my wife, Chris."

"Pleased to meet you. Tommy Kennedy." He shook our hands. He was a graying man with a little mustache and bright blue eyes, a little heavier than he should have been, but I guessed he didn't get much exercise. He wore a regulation security uniform, dark blue pants, light blue shirt, dark blue tie, the blue jacket of which hung from a hook on an old-fashioned brown wooden coat tree. A rather fancy watch, with a lot of dials and numbers, sat on a hairy left wrist, and he looked at it often as we talked as though it was new or he was concerned about the time. "You talkin' about that one where they found the lady's body over near the fence?"

"That's the one," I said. "Do you remember it?"

"Nah. Wasn't here then. I only been here about ten years. I'm retired from the job. You're still on the job, ain't ya?" he said to Jack.

"Yes. The Six-Five in Brooklyn."

"Brooklyn, yeah. I worked in Manhattan all my life."

"How do you know about it, then?" I asked.

"They all talked about it, told me when I started to work here. The guy before me, he was workin' here when they found the body. I guess he never forgot it, biggest thing ever happened to him."

"You remember his name?"

"Sure. Pete Crowley. He's dead now, don't go lookin' for him. Died a coupla years ago. That happened way back, didn't it?"

"About sixteen years ago."

"There might be someone from back then," he said. "One of the night guys has been here about twenty years, but you won't find him over a weekend. Juan Castro's his name. He'll tell you about it."

"When does he work?"

"Four to twelve, Monday through Friday. Never misses a day."

"Did you ever hear of anyone named Handleman working here?" I asked on a sudden whim.

"Handleman? Here? Never knew a Handleman in my life. Doesn't mean he didn't work here. Ask Castro. He'll tell you."

We said our good-byes and started to go, but Mr. Kennedy was now interested in old times on the job. There wasn't much he and Jack had in common. Jack had become a police officer about the time Kennedy had retired, but the older man kept us there as he asked questions that showed his heart was still on the old job. Finally we stepped out into the cold air.

"Hot as hell in there," Jack said.

"I suppose he makes rounds and then he's glad to come back to the warmth."

"I'd fall asleep."

"He probably does, too. I guess no one'll ever forget the day they found poor Iris."

"You find a body, it's a day you remember the rest of your life. Let me show you how fast you can get from here to the Grand Concourse."

We got in the car and drove back to Broadway, then north across the short bridge over the Spuyten Duyvil River. To the left were the luxury apartment houses of the southwest Bronx with their magnificent views of the Hudson, the George Washington Bridge, and the Palisades of New Jersey. We had hardly crossed the river when Jack made a right turn. We crossed over the Major Deegan Expressway, which runs along the east side of the Harlem River and then through Van Cortlandt Park where it becomes the New York State Thruway. In a minute we were driving under the elevated train at Jerome Avenue and then up a little hill to the Grand Concourse.

"Aunt Sylvie lives right over there," I said, pointing left. "One of those buildings. You're right. It's not far at all. A jogger could do it in no time."

"So there it is, another possibility. Let's go home and

clean up the yard. While we're at it, I'd like to take some measurements and see about that family room."

I suddenly had the feeling that it was in the works.

20

On the way home we stopped at a hardware store and bought a hundred-foot metal tape measure. Then we went home and used it. The house I inherited from Aunt Meg is not large, three bedrooms on the second floor, a kitchen, living room, and dining room on the first. But the property is more than ample, and even with the garage behind and detached from the house, there's a lot of land back there. The dimensions Jack was thinking about, and measuring for, would build the largest room in the house and still hardly make a dent in our backyard.

"How do you like it?" he asked as he planted the last stake at the last corner.

"It's awfully big," I said, not echoing his enthusiasm for the project.

"You worried about what it's going to cost?"

"I'm scared to death."

"We're the only people I know who don't have a mortgage and don't pay rent."

"But we pay taxes, Jack, and they're high. They're very high. And they'll be a lot higher if we add onto the house. I earn very little, don't forget."

"But I earn plenty and I've been putting money away for years."

"You have?"

"I showed you the bankbook before we got married."

"I guess I didn't really look. I was so overwhelmed by your character and personality."

"And my incomparable good looks."

"That, too," I said, trying not to smile. If he was losing his mind, someone had to stay in control, and there didn't seem to be anyone else around.

"Now here's what I'm thinking." He moved out of the rectangle as though the structure had already been built. "It probably wouldn't cost all that much more to put a second floor on it."

"Jack, really. I think—this is really getting out of hand."

"That'll give us a huge bedroom with room for a big closet and maybe a master bathroom. If we work it right, we can—"

"Jack, I think I'm going to faint."

"Are you kidding me?"

"No, really, I feel a little light-headed. This is just terrifying me."

He crossed the invisible wall, which I was now certain I would never allow to be built, and put his arm around me. "It's OK, honey. I promise you we won't do anything we can't afford. The taxes we pay here are really just a drop in the bucket."

"When I was living here alone they seemed enormous."

"Because you weren't earning much and you really don't have any idea what most people pay to live."

"Marilyn said her father was paying less than a hundred a month when he moved into that apartment on Seventy-first Street."

"Chris, that was the nineteen thirties. It was the Depression. Do you have any idea what it would go for now on the open market?"

"I suppose close to a thousand."

"Fifteen hundred. And if they fix up the kitchen and bathroom—"

"Bathrooms," I interjected.

"Bathrooms! Hell, two thousand right off the bat."

"Well," I said.

"You still feel light-headed?"

"More. It doesn't seem possible. How can people afford it?"

"The point is, we can afford a lot more than we're paying. And if we moved into the big bedroom, we can put the baby in the one we're sleeping in now."

"The baby? Jack, do you know something I don't know?"

"Well, we're gonna have one, aren't we?"

"Yes, sure. I guess so."

"And if we wait till it's born to start doing anything to the house, it'll be a real mess around here while they're building. You don't want that with a new baby, do you?"

"No, of course not. Why do I feel as though I missed a very important conversation somewhere along the way?"

"We didn't have it. I thought it would be best to present you with a complete plan so you'd know it wasn't just a pipe dream."

"Do you know what this plan of yours is going to cost?"

"I have a pretty good idea, yeah."

"You've talked to people?"

"I've talked to people. I haven't got any firm estimates yet, but I know what it'll cost."

"These things always cost more than you think," I said as though I knew what I was talking about.

"I know that, too."

"I've never been in debt."

"Don't think of it as debt. Think of it as rent. Think of it as an investment. We want to live here, don't we?"

I nodded.

"And we want a family."

I nodded.

"So we'll build a little addition on the house, which will make it the greatest house we've ever lived in and we'll have our baby and we'll be happy ever after."

I nodded.

"I love you, Chris."

Tears started down my cheeks.

"It's OK, baby," he said. "I promise you. Everything'll be great." He kissed me.

"The neighbors will see," I said hoarsely.

"Don't they know we're married?"

"Most of them, I guess."

"Come on inside. And don't step on the family room floor."

Eileen called later in the afternoon and read a draft of a letter she was writing to Taffy.

"You write drafts first?" I said.

"Well, I've gone through about a hundred different ways of saying what I think I want to say and I was off base on the first try."

"I'm listening."

She read it with the emotion I knew she was feeling, referring to their long friendship, their years of shared experiences, and the genuine affection she had for Taffy, which she knew was returned. It took a couple of paragraphs to say it and then Eileen cleared her throat and launched into a clear statement of forgiveness. When she had finished reading it to me, she said, "The problem is, it's incomplete. I haven't said anything about us getting back together."

"Do you want to do it this soon?"

"I don't know."

"Have you decided what you want to do?"

"I'm not sure."

"You can always send what you've got, Eileen. It's beautifully written and very touching. I think she'll be relieved and happy to get it."

"But it begs the question."

She was right. "If you send the letter as it's written, without mentioning her question or giving an answer, she'll understand that you haven't come to a decision yet."

"Chris, could you talk to her for me?"

"I couldn't do that, Eileen," I said before I knew the words were out of my mouth.

"I'm sorry. I shouldn't have asked."

I felt terrible. This was Jack's sister and she had done so much for us, been so good to us. I wanted very much to be her friend, to have a warm, happy relationship with her, and here I had snapped out an answer to an important question and left her hanging. "It's not that I don't want to," I said rather lamely. "I know what I'm good at. I'm not a mediator. I don't have the skills and I don't have the temperament."

"Your temperament is fine. Look, please don't feel you have to apologize. I was just trying to pass a difficult task off to you because I'm afraid of doing it myself. Let me work on the letter a little more and I'll call you back."

"Eileen, let me think about this. I answered without thinking."

"No," she said. "What you said was right. This is my problem. I'll talk to you after I have something else on paper."

I really felt awful. It was true it was her problem, but it was one she had not made for herself. It had happened to her because she had trusted one of the people in the world she had most reason to trust.

I went out for a walk and ran into Mel and Marilyn just getting out of a car.

"Come on in," Mel said. "We're about to have some coffee and good stuff. Mom brought a treat."

"And we can talk," Marilyn said, giving me a kiss. "Come on in, dear."

We settled in the family room and I took a careful look around from my new perspective. Jack hadn't talked about a fireplace, but I could imagine he had one in mind, and at the cost I'd heard people mention, I was on the verge of hyperventilating again. But this room was wonderful, comfortable, warm, the kind of place where you could spread out and stretch out. If only it didn't mean debt and large monthly payments . . .

"Has anything turned up?" Marilyn asked.

"Only in theory," I said. I told her about my trip to St. Stephen's and Joseph's comments.

"Somebody gave something to her," Marilyn said thoughtfully. "Then why did he kill her?"

"Maybe they had a fight over the gift and he wanted it back, maybe because she was going away to Europe and wouldn't be able to see him for a long time."

"A lover?"

"I just don't know. Anything's possible. And we could have been right the first time. Maybe the killer was a grown child that she'd been supporting and she decided enough was enough."

"We must be missing a lot of facts, Chris."

"We are. I'm sure your father knows many of the relevant ones, but I understand why you can't ask him and I don't want to try."

"He's moving back to the apartment today. I got someone to stay with him. My sister is taking him over. I'll visit him tomorrow, stock up his refrigerator, do some cooking for him."

"Don't ask him, Marilyn. If this investigation has upset him as much as it seems to, let it lie. Maybe Arnold Gold will turn up something. Maybe Jack and I will come up with something. I'm going to try to see Mrs. Garganus again. She rushed me out of there because she didn't want me to ask about Iris. That woman knows something we need to know."

"I hope you can think of the right question to ask."

"This is going to come together, Marilyn. I feel it. All these bits and pieces are going to give us an answer. I just need one or two more bits to make it happen."

"I'll look around the apartment tomorrow."

"Please don't. I mean that. Your father will know if something's been disturbed, and this is not the time to alienate him. He needs you so much. His life is more important than Iris's death."

"I know. I just can't help thinking he's going to destroy something very valuable tonight."

"Then let him. I want to talk to Sylvie face-to-face again. I'm sure she told me there was someone new in Iris's life after Harry. She's holding something back, and maybe I can persuade her to give it to me."

"If we could just find Shirley Finster," Marilyn said.

It was what I wanted, too. Maybe Sylvie, I thought. Maybe she knew.

I told Jack about Eileen's call and her request. "I feel bad, but I turned her down," I said. "I wish I hadn't, but I said it without thinking."

"Don't feel bad. It's not your place to put yourself between them and take the flak. If Eileen wants someone to talk to Taffy, I will. Taffy's a felon. And worse than that, she's a rotten friend."

"I don't think you should talk to her. You're very angry with her."

"Shouldn't I be?"

"Yes, you should. But Eileen feels so bad about this that I'm sure she doesn't want her big brother marching in like a cop and telling Taffy where to get off."

"Taffy should do time. Eileen should go to the DA and press charges."

"That's between her and the law. The rest of it is between her and Taffy. Eileen has to do this her way."

"But she shouldn't get you involved."

"Let's not worry about it."

* * *

I woke up with a start in the middle of the night, coming out of a nightmare that seemed to incorporate everything that was on my mind, Iris's murder, Eileen's trouble, and the family room. My heart was pounding with fear and I had a feeling I would not get back to sleep easily. I slipped out of bed and stuck my feet in my sneakers, grabbed my robe and left the bedroom. There was perfect silence as I went down the stairs in the dark, holding on to the banister and feeling my way. The only light came in from the door, and that wasn't very much.

I sat on the sofa for a few minutes while I calmed down. I couldn't remember ever feeling this way except when people were sick, my mother when I was in high school and my Aunt Meg only a couple of years ago. But those were very different times from these. I was much happier now than when I was a teenager, and far more secure. And during the time that Aunt Meg was ill, I was coincidentally going through my own difficult time as a nun, working out what I wanted to do with my life, negotiating a break that would change my life even more than entering St. Stephen's had.

My heart having quieted, I got up and took my coat out of the closet, stuck my key in my pocket, and went outside. It was freezing cold and I almost went back in again, but instead I walked up the driveway to the back of the house and gazed in the dark at the winter lawn that would return to life in a matter of weeks, the shrubs along the back of the house that Aunt Meg had nurtured every spring and summer, the big trees that I could hardly see along the far boundary of the property. I could remember some of them when they were hardly as tall as I was then. What I couldn't make out in the dark was the little peach tree my next-door neighbors had given me before Jack and I were married. Imagine having a tree that bore peaches! Tucked away in my file was a recipe for peach pie that Mel had given me. Maybe this would be the summer the crop would be large enough to bake one.

A person's life leaves an imprint on a house. Aunt Meg's was on this one so strongly that perhaps I had been too intimidated to begin to leave my own. Every tree and shrub, every blade of grass, every piece of furniture and rug and appliance, was hers. Even the dishes and glasses and cutlery had been left to me. When we married, we had moved Jack's bed into our bedroom and brought his desk and a few odds and ends along. But something in me had been very reluctant to make major changes.

Was I afraid of something? In the convent, when a nun died, her clothes were given over to other nuns of her size. Her bed and desk and dresser became another's furniture. In a way that now troubled me, I had moved into my aunt's house and assumed her possessions with no thought of putting my own stamp on the house. Was it custom or fear or simply that I did not know how? Or was I afraid of losing Aunt Meg in the transformation?

"Chris?"

"I'm back here."

He came around the corner of the house in his bathrobe and slippers. "You scared hell out of me," he said, putting his arm around me.

"I'm fine. I just woke up and didn't feel like sleeping. You must be freezing."

"I am."

I put my arms around him. "Let's go in."

"Is it the family room that's troubling you?"

"It's everything. It's Iris and Eileen and my own pigheadedness."

"Being afraid of something isn't being pigheaded. I know where you're coming from. You've never spent money and everything looks like a lot."

"When the college gave me my first paycheck, I looked around for someone to give it to."

"I know, honey. And you don't want a new car and you take tuna fish sandwiches with you because they're cheaper than a coffee shop. The only one you spend money on is me."

"Well, you're worth it."

"But you're worth it, too."

"It's not just the money, Jack." I slipped my arm around his waist and walked him over behind the house, passing the stakes he had left in the ground. "Aunt Meg spent so much time on that garden. Her bulbs come up in the spring like magic, the perennials never forget to bloom. If we add onto the house, I'm afraid we'll lose that and I'll lose part of her gift to me."

"Then we'll move them. I don't think the bulbs are a problem. We can get the guy from the Oakwood Nursery to move the bigger stuff like the shrubs."

"That would be nice." Something weighty inside me dissolved. "I think Gene would miss those things, too, when he came to visit."

"We'll keep them. There's lots of land here. We can find a good place for everything."

"I don't want to lose her," I said.

"We'll move slowly."

"OK."

"And we won't spend too much. There are things I

can do myself. My dad put a hammer in my hand at an early age."

"I can paint. I painted at St. Stephen's."

"You never told me."

We started walking back to the driveway. "It was easier than cooking," I admitted.

"Who picked the paint?"

"Probably Sister Clare Angela. She was the Superior at the time. I think she got a deal from the hardware store." We went into the house.

"Man, it was cold out there."

"Want some hot chocolate?"

"Why not? I suppose you wouldn't consider skipping mass."

"I'll think about it."

"That's pretty open-minded of you."

"I'm a pretty open-minded person."

"You are. You know that?"

I kissed his cold cheek. "Except where debt's concerned. Then I'm pigheaded."

"I'll deal with it. Make me my cocoa."

21

Marilyn called Sunday evening. "I've been with Pop most of the day," she said. "He's weaker than he was last time I saw him. And a lot thinner."

"I'm sorry to hear it. This must be very difficult for you."

"Think how difficult it is for him."

"Yes. Is he comfortable in the apartment?"

"Actually, he's a lot more comfortable than he was at my sister's. I think he was right to go home."

"It's nice to be in your own home."

"He wants to talk to you, Chris. Would you be willing to go into New York tomorrow?"

"Sure."

I wasn't looking forward to it. I wanted to remember him as I had seen him at the seder when his grip on my arm had been strong and he had been in control as the senior member of the family. But if he wanted to see me, I was certainly not going to deny him.

Since we were driving into the city, I called Sylvie and asked if we could talk again. She said yes, I could come over, and we set up a time.

When I got off the phone, I told Jack about my appointments. "If we finish late enough, I think I'll ask

Marilyn to drive up to the oil yards and see if I can talk to Juan Castro."

"Tell him to walk you back to your car. I don't want you up there in the dark with just another woman."

"I will."

"That's a busy day for you, three interviews. You bucking for a gold shield?"

"Just a break in this case soon or it's all over. I want Sylvie—or Mr. Grodnik—to give me Shirley Finster's name and address. I don't think he will, but maybe Sylvie can be persuaded."

"What about the Garganus angle?"

"Maybe Tuesday after my class. I'd like to be there when her granddaughter comes home from school. Erin might just let me into the house before her grandmother knows what's happening."

"Get 'em while they're vulnerable."

"Brooks's rule?"

"Everybody's rule."

"I'll take it under advisement."

A stout woman with a nice smile opened the door of the Grodnik apartment. "Come in, Mrs. Margulies," she said, and smiled at me, too. "He's in the living room, all dressed and ready to see you."

Marilyn introduced Mrs. Hires and me, then we hung up our coats and went to see her father.

"You look good, Pop," Marilyn said. "You sleep well?"

"Pretty good. I don't sleep the way I used to."

"None of us do. Here's Chris."

He held out his hand and we shook. The hand was thin, but the grip was firm.

"It's nice to see you again, Mr. Grodnik."

"We have some talking to do. Make yourself comfortable. Marilyn." He turned to his daughter. "Sit down somewhere. Stop looking around as if you could find a speck of dust. Just sit and let us talk. You can listen, but try not to butt in."

I had a feeling he wanted to make sure she wouldn't leave the room and start to look for missing papers, but however she felt, she sat obediently.

"Christine," he said, turning to me, "you enjoyed the seder?"

"It was a wonderful experience. I'm grateful to have had the opportunity."

"When I was a boy my mother used to invite people who didn't have a place to go for Passover. Sometimes a man would come over from the old country and leave his family behind until he could save enough to have them join him. There were always a couple of men I didn't know well at our seders. Well, I'm glad you enjoyed it. My daughter told me you had a beautiful wedding last summer."

"Very beautiful, and thanks to her. Marilyn helped me with a lot of things I couldn't have done alone."

"Marilyn is good that way. All my children are good people. My wife and I did the best we could for them, and they all went on and did better. I leave a better world than I came into."

"You're part of a better world," I said.

"Yes, for a little while, maybe. I understand you are trying to find out who killed my little sister, Iris."

"I've been looking into it."

"The police never found the killer."

"I've talked to the detective, Mr. Grodnik. That case is open and it still bothers him after all these years."

"Unfinished business. Everybody feels the same about unfinished business. I don't think you'll find a killer. It's a long time ago, people move around, the snow melts and the footprints disappear."

"We found Iris's pocketbook in your front closet."

"Marilyn told me." He smiled. "That closet. Nobody ever looked in there. Maybe you could find a million dollars in there if you looked hard enough. Where is the pocketbook now?"

"I gave it to the police."

"What was in it?"

I wondered if that was the reason for this meeting. He might be afraid that an address book or a checkbook had been inside it, giving information that he wanted to keep to himself.

"Her keys, her lipstick, her wallet, her credit cards, a little date book. Not much else."

"So it didn't help."

"It told us she was planning to come back to the seder. She had no money with her and no keys."

"I see. So you think she went downstairs to say hello to an old friend and the old friend killed her."

"I think it was something like that. Do you happen to have Iris's address book?"

"Why should I have her address book?"

"Because when Iris's apartment was cleaned out, her things must have been taken somewhere. I thought maybe they came here."

"Some of them did, but I don't remember an address book."

"I'd like to get in touch with her friend Shirley Finster."

"Shirley," he said. "I remember Shirley."

"Do you know how I can find her?"

"I wouldn't have any idea. But I remember Shirley when she was a little girl. She was a good friend to my sister."

"Did Shirley marry?"

"It's possible."

I sat back in my chair. This meeting had been at his request. If he wanted to tell me something, he knew how to do it. From the little I had asked, it was clear he wasn't going to answer the questions I needed answered.

"What I don't understand," he said after a moment, "is why you are looking into something that has nothing to do with you."

"I asked her to, Pop," Marilyn said. "You know that. I told you."

"But you," he said, looking at me. "What makes you so interested?"

"Homicides are interesting. I've worked on a few since I moved to Oakwood."

"Do you know something now about my sister's murder that I don't know?"

"I know that Iris quit her job about a week before the seder."

"She quit her job? Who told you this?"

"The company she worked for, GAR."

"It can't be true."

"It is true, Pop," Marilyn said.

"She never told us."

I didn't say anything.

"There's more?" he asked.

"She may have been planning a trip to Europe."

"This I don't know either."

"Switzerland," I added.

"Switzerland is a nice country, I hear. How do you know these things?"

"I talked to Mrs. Garganus, her boss's wife. She knew that Iris was going to Europe."

"Her boss's wife knew something her family didn't know?"

"I'm sure she would have told you before she left. Maybe she was just making plans. She had a date in her book for a bridal shower after Passover. I think she intended to leave after that."

"She was going with Shirley?" he asked.

"I don't know. If I could find Shirley, I would ask her."

"You know something about this, Marilyn?"

"Just what Chris told me. You never heard about it?"

"Never. Iris spent the whole day with your mother before the seder. She never said a word. You think maybe she was going with that boyfriend?"

"Harry?" Marilyn said. "She wasn't seeing Harry anymore."

"Harry didn't know about the trip," I said.

"You talked to Harry, too?" Abraham Grodnik said, his surprise apparent.

"We talked last week. He saw Iris once in a while and he talked to her on the phone. She didn't tell him."

"So she was saving it for a surprise. It would have been nice, a trip to the mountains, some good fresh air. She deserved a trip like that. You know anything else?"

"I know Iris was married," I said.

His eyebrows went up and his shoulders moved. "Married," he said disdainfully. "Married is when two people live together and have a family, not when you put someone's ring on your finger because he has a pretty face. Iris's marriage lasted fifteen minutes. There was nothing to it. It broke my mother's heart. She was a young girl. She didn't know any better. It was a marriage like they have in Hollywood."

"Did she stay friends with him?" I asked.

"Friends? She never saw him again. He went to the war."

"Did he come back?"

"Maybe he came back. I don't remember."

He was starting to look tired, and I felt uneasy about staying. I had told him what I knew, and he had added nothing. I didn't think that staying longer would change that. The effects of his disease were all over his face and body, and I didn't want our presence to drain his energy further.

"It was nice of you to come," he said, taking the initiative. "Talking makes me tired. If you find out anything else, I hope you'll let me know."

"I will," I said, standing.

"Iris was a very independent woman," he said, his eyes closed. "From the day she was born, she did what she wanted. Usually she got what she wanted, too, but not always. She didn't get Harry. It's too bad. Harry was a nice man. She could have had a good life with him, even with her problems." He closed his eyes.

Marilyn went over and ruffled his hair, then bent and kissed his forehead. I touched his arm and we left the living room, walking up the two steps to the foyer.

"He's asleep," Marilyn said to Mrs. Hires.

"Well, it's no wonder he's tired. He had a big morning."

"Did he go to the doctor?"

"Oh no. We didn't leave the apartment. He spent the morning cleaning up."

"Cleaning up what?"

"Throwing away junk." She pulled out the drawer of a secretary that stood in the foyer. It was nearly empty. "He took everything out, looked at it, put it in the garbage, a box, some loose papers, a lot of stuff. It took an hour, I'm sure."

"Do you have the papers?" Marilyn asked.

"He made me go out to the incinerator and throw it all away."

"I guess he's done it then," Marilyn said. She took a deep breath. "Come on, Chris. Let's have some lunch."

We walked down the hallway to the elevator and I stopped and pulled open the door to the incinerator, just on the chance that something was there, an envelope, a slip of paper that had fallen to the floor. But the room was clean except for a cigarette butt. Mrs. Hires had done her job well. The papers Abraham Grodnik wanted destroyed were gone.

22

"This must be very hard for you," I said after we had been shown to a table in a small Italian restaurant.

"It is." She looked as if the visit had worn her out. "I think I'll have a drink for a change. How about you, Chris?"

"A glass of white wine."

She ordered Scotch for herself and she sipped it before speaking again. "He's gotten rid of everything," she said. "How can he not want us to find out who killed his sister?"

"Maybe that's not what he threw away. Maybe it's documents that show Iris had a child or went to jail or had a second marriage."

"Iris didn't go to jail." She picked up the menu and looked at it briefly. "I'll have their pasta and salad," she said. "They'll put any sauce on that you ask for."

"Sounds good."

We picked different sauces and different salad dressings and sipped our different drinks.

"I offered yesterday to move in with him, but he wouldn't have it. He said everything was fine just the way it is."

"He's a very independent man. You're like him, Marilyn."

"I suppose I am. He looked terrible, didn't he?"

"I haven't seen him since the seder, and he looked thinner to me. Paler, too, I think."

"He doesn't get out much. If he would come and stay with me ... Well, this doesn't get us anywhere. He's not going to change at his age. He seemed genuinely surprised when you told him Iris had been planning a trip."

"He was. I'm sure he'd never heard about it before."

"Did you notice how he shrugged off her marriage? Just tossed it out as though everyone had always known about it? That secret was kept from me my entire life until just now."

"Maybe it doesn't seem quite so important to him anymore."

"But something was important enough to throw in the garbage before we came."

"Marilyn, maybe we should set this all aside. Your father's illness is enough for you to worry about."

"The truth is, thinking about this takes my mind off the other. I rather enjoy this little bit of intrigue. You don't want to stop, do you?"

"No. I want to find Shirley Finster."

"Well, Pop's not giving anything away. Let's hope Sylvie does."

We took our time with lunch and then headed up to the Bronx. Sylvie was my last hope, too.

"Marilyn, I wasn't expecting you," Sylvie said, a trifle disappointed, I thought.

"I had to go in to see Pop, and Chris said she was

coming here, so we just got together in one car. I'll sit in the bedroom, dear. I'm not going to bother you."

"Well, take a magazine with you." Sylvie picked up a couple that were on the sofa and handed them to Marilyn. When Marilyn had left us, we sat at the kitchen table where a pot of tea was waiting and a box of cookies.

"I used to go to the bakery and buy good cookies," Sylvie said, pouring tea, "but the bakeries closed down a long time ago. Nothing's the same."

"These are fine. How are you feeling?"

"So-so." She sipped her tea and ate a cookie.

"Sylvie, when I was here the first time, you told me Iris had a new boyfriend."

"Did I?"

"I think you did. Did you ever meet him?"

"I never met anyone after Harry."

"Are you sure she had a boyfriend?"

"She would say she had to meet someone, she was busy, someone was visiting her. Who else could it be?"

"I don't know. Is it possible she had a child back when she was married and he found her later and came to see her?"

"Iris? A child? Iris never had a child. I saw Iris all the time. You can't hide something that big. And she was very small. I would have known."

"And you don't think she was mixed up with Mr. Garganus?"

"Never."

"Sylvie, did you ever own a car?"

"Me? Never. But my son did. Bought it with his own money when he was in college."

"Was he at the seder when Iris died?"

"Oh, he was gone by then. He didn't live in New York anymore."

So much for a quick trip down from the Bronx. "What about Iris's friend Shirley Finster? Do you think you could find an address for her?"

"Oh, Shirley, yes. After I finish my tea I'll have a look."

That was the end of our conversation. Sylvie started talking about other things, her children, her late husband, her friend who lived in Florida. I worried that she would intentionally forget to look for Shirley's address, and I didn't know whether to suggest that Marilyn be invited to join us since we had stopped talking about Iris.

But she didn't forget. When she finished her cup, she said, "Let's go look," and I followed her to the back of the apartment. "Marilyn?" she called. "Go into the kitchen and have some tea. Chris and I are looking for something."

"Finished already?" Marilyn said, opening the door of the bedroom.

"Almost," Sylvie said. "There's cookies and tea. You know where the cups are."

Sylvie went right to her closet and pulled out a box that was on the floor. Dust covered the top and she made a sound of annoyance but didn't bother to remove it. She took the top off and laid it carefully on the floor without disturbing the dust. The box was square and was marked "Bergdorf Goodman," and I guessed it had belonged to her sister.

"I have a few of Iris's things here. Let me see if the address book is there." She poked around without finding anything, then began to remove mementos of her sister, envelopes of photos, a silk scarf, a small hat with a veil that must have come from the forties or fifties, a leather belt, a framed picture of an unsmiling couple in clothes from early in the century. "My parents," she said, looking at it for a moment. "I should keep it out, shouldn't I?" She put it on her dresser and came back to the box.

"This is the book she kept by the telephone," she said, pulling out a worn binder about four by six inches. "Let's see if Shirley's in it." She flipped to *F* and I saw her run her finger down the page. "I don't see it here," she said.

"Maybe it's under her married name."

"I don't remember her married name."

"Could I look through the book?"

Sylvie shook her head. "I guess it's not here."

"She might have put it under the *S*'s."

She flipped the pages. "Oh, there's lots of *S*'s here. Let's see. You're right, Chris. Shirley. It's the first one on the page."

I had my pencil handy. "That's wonderful, Sylvie. Is the last name there?"

"Finster Mandelbaum. Three seven eight Prince Street, Teaneck, New Jersey. And here's the phone number." She recited it, then closed the book. "I guess you came to the right place." She smiled and put the book in a dresser drawer.

"Thank you very much, Sylvie."

"Don't say I didn't help you now."

"You've been a big help. I really appreciate it."

"Let's have some more tea."

* * *

"So it was there all along," Marilyn said. "And she knew it, didn't she?"

"She went right to the box. I wonder what changed her mind."

"Sylvie's a funny one. She's always been that way. Sometimes you think you can push her around, make her do whatever you want her to, and other times she's as stubborn as my father. Maybe she liked you. Maybe she found out Shirley's been dead for years so it didn't hurt to give you the information."

"I'll call her tonight." I looked at my watch. "Marilyn, I know this isn't on our itinerary for today, but it's almost four and the four-to-twelve security guard at the oil yards comes on soon. Would you mind driving over there? It's not far and I'd like to talk to him."

"Why not?"

I directed her and she was surprised at how close the yards were.

"I thought someone in Sylvie's family might have driven by the oil yards and knew where they were."

"And killed Iris? I don't think so. Her son's a nice person. He was living up in Boston around that time. What would ever make him want to kill Iris?"

"Somebody must have had a reason."

She parked the car just as the security guards changed. We waited until the early one left, then walked over to the shack. I knocked.

"Come on in."

The man inside was a handsome Hispanic in his mid-forties, tall with skin that looked lightly tanned and a build that he took care of. "Help you ladies?"

I introduced us and started to tell him why we were there.

"I think I'll wait outside," Marilyn said. "The heat's a little too much for me."

"I won't be long," I promised.

"It is pretty warm, isn't it? But after my rounds, it's nice to come back inside. You were saying about the body."

"Did you find her?"

"Well, I heard the dog barking. I was on my rounds and realized there was a lot of noise. I went over to see what was wrong and I saw the body."

"What was your first impression?" I asked.

"That she'd been dead for a while, that she'd been beaten. I didn't have a cellular phone at that time, so I ran back to the shack and called the police. The two kids with the dog were pretty shook up, and I told them to come around and sit in my shack. The cops came pretty quick."

"You're here from four to twelve?"

"Yeah."

"I guess you don't know if her body was dumped during your tour."

"Coulda been on mine, coulda been on the next guy's. I don't think it happened during the day."

"Had you ever seen her before?"

"Never. You better believe the cops talked to me for a long time."

"Is there anyone who worked here who could have known her?"

"You mean like the other security guards? It's possible, but I don't think so. One of those guys is dead now. The other retired."

"Do most of you hold this job for a long time?"

"Most, yeah, but not all. We have guys come on and they just can't take it. Some of them last a week, some of them last a year. They just find out it's not for them and they quit."

"Do any names come back to you, Mr. Castro? People that might have worked here around the time the body was found or just before that?"

"That's a tough one," he said. "Going back that far. There was a guy named Mauer or something like that. Stayed maybe six months. I remember him because he was taking courses during the day, and that's what I do. But he got a degree and left."

I wrote the name down, mostly because it began with *M*. "Anyone else?"

"Uh, guy named Scott was here for a while, midnight to eight. There was a Gordon, a Giordano. I couldn't tell you if they were here before or after, but none of them lasted. You have to have a certain temperament to work midnight to eight. It's not easy."

"I couldn't do it myself," I admitted. "What kind of courses do you take?"

"I took a degree. Now I'm working on my M.B.A. Someday I'll go into business for myself." He smiled. He was a handsome man with perfect teeth.

"Thank you for your time."

"It's nice to talk to someone. You got any more questions, I'm here Monday through Friday."

I thanked him again and went outside. Marilyn was standing near the sidewalk.

"Get anything?"

"I don't think so, but I had to ask. Does the name Mauer mean anything to you?"

"No."

"Nobody Iris ever knew?"

"Not that she told me about."

We got in the car. "Well, there's Shirley Finster Mandelbaum and a return trip to Mrs. Garganus."

"And then all the leads are dry."

"I'm afraid so."

"Mauer," she said. "I'll think about it."

23

Hoping Shirley was still at the same number, I dialed it and a man answered. "May I speak to Mrs. Mandelbaum?" I said.

"Who is this?"

"Christine Bennett."

"Are you selling something?"

It was that time of night, not long after the dinner hour, and I didn't blame him for asking. "No I'm not. It's a personal call."

"Just a minute."

The sounds were not intelligible, but a moment later a thin female voice said, "Hello?"

"Mrs. Mandelbaum, my name is Christine Bennett."

"Could you speak up, please? I don't hear too well."

I repeated my name louder. "Iris Grodnik's niece, Marilyn, asked me to look into her murder."

"Oh, you're the one Sylvie said would be calling."

So Sylvie had gotten there first. "Sylvie gave me your name this afternoon. I wonder if I could come over and talk to you."

"It would be a wasted trip. I don't know what I could tell you. Iris was my best friend since kindergarten. I told the police everything I knew, which was nothing.

They said she was downstairs in the street the night of the seder and someone came along and took her away. They never found him."

"Mrs. Mandelbaum, did Iris know anyone whose name was Mauer?"

"Bauer?" she said.

"No, Mauer." I spelled it for her.

"She never told me. But she had friends at work, and there were people she knew in the building she lived in."

"Did she talk to you about her boss?"

"Mr. Garganus? She loved him."

"Do you mean he was her boyfriend?"

"Oh no." She laughed a tinkly little laugh. "I mean she thought he was a wonderful man to work for."

"Did you know Iris quit her job about a week before she was killed?"

There was a silence. I had hit her with a tough question. I clung to the phone, hoping she would say something new, something I hadn't heard from anyone else. "She didn't really quit," she said hesitantly. "She expected to go back."

I felt a rush of success. "But she told you she was leaving GAR for a while."

"She told me. It was a little sudden. She was going away somewhere. She was—she was doing a favor for someone."

"Do you know for whom? Or where she was going?"

"Maybe she was going to Europe. When she told me, it wasn't settled yet."

"Do you know who she was doing the favor for?"

"I couldn't tell you, Miss—"

"Chris. Chris Bennett. Mrs. Mandelbaum, someone

murdered your best friend. I want to bring him to justice."

"They didn't kill her," she said mysteriously. "They were good people. Iris told me things she didn't tell anyone else because we were such good friends and she trusted me to keep a secret. It isn't right for me to say what it was. It had nothing to do with her, believe me. It was just a favor she was doing."

"Mrs. Mandelbaum, do you have a pencil? I'd like to give you my phone number."

"There's nothing more I can tell you. It won't bring Iris back and it could hurt somebody who doesn't deserve it."

"Please write it down," I said. I dictated the number, then said my name again.

"OK," she said lightly. "It's right here where I'll see it. Maybe I'll think of something."

"Thank you." It wasn't a matter of thinking of something; it was deciding to tell me. I had been right about her. She knew everything.

Eileen called before Jack came home. "Feeling any better?" I asked.

"I do. I've heard from Taffy. I think we have to talk, and we can't do this over the phone."

"I agree. Being in the same room would be better. If you think you can manage it."

"I think we can. Could we use your living room?"

I took a breath before answering. "Sure. Do you want me here or should I get in my car and disappear?"

"I'd like you there, Chris. Will you do it?"

"Yes."

"I'll get back to you and we'll make an appointment.

I know you teach on Tuesday so we'll make it some other day. I don't want my brother around. He goes ballistic when I mention Taffy."

"I know what you mean. It's because he has your best interests at heart."

"Whatever. We'll make it a weekday."

I told her I would be available.

I made a quick call before I left for the college on Tuesday morning. Cathy Holloway came on the line and I told her who I was.

"Yes, Chris. How are you? Have you found out who killed Iris?"

"Not yet, but I've dug up a lot of old information. I wanted to ask you about the Garganuses' son."

"They had a son?" she said. "Are you sure?"

"Well, I thought they did. You think they didn't?"

"They had a daughter. I never heard about a son."

"I see."

"It was very tragic. They tried to hush it up, but I'm pretty sure she committed suicide. She was a girl with a lot of problems. Some of the older people here had heard gossip."

"Would you share it with me?"

"Just that when she was younger she was troubled, alcohol, drugs, the usual."

I swallowed hard at her characterization of the daughter's troubles. "Do you remember when she died?"

"Five or six years ago. It could be more. I think Mr. Garganus died about a year later. It really broke him up. He tried very hard with her. Both of them did."

"Was she their only child?"

"I never heard of any other. Unless there's a son I don't know about."

"I may be wrong on that, Cathy. But thanks very much. You've got me thinking along a new line, and that may be for the best." I looked at my watch, said a quick good-bye, and ran off to teach my class.

We were talking about the English Romantic poets that morning, and I always enjoyed the reactions of my female students to some of the sentiments that group of poets expressed. Shelley's frequent weeping did not go over well with most classes, but *Ozymandias* held its own. Keats, my personal favorite, fared better, especially when they realized how young he was when he died, an age that most of them would achieve in a few years and I had left behind. It's always a pleasure when they discover a wonderful line whose origin was unknown until they opened their book and found it there. "Beauty is truth," "the alien corn," "Here lies one whose name was writ in water," and my favorite, "Heard melodies are sweet, but those unheard are sweeter." When we read and discuss some of these poems, I see a lot of smiles on otherwise sullen or neutral faces, which accounts for a lot of my joy in teaching this course.

I had a satisfying lunch in the cafeteria, sampling the products of the food service department. While they sometimes forgot to salt the soup, an easily remedied oversight, their food was always well prepared and interesting, and I treated myself to a wedge of warm blueberry pie for dessert.

The poems were still ringing in my ear as I drove to New York. I let my mind wander beyond the words and the sentiments, resting for a while on Eileen and Taffy and Taffy's sister, on Shirley Finster Mandelbaum, who may have given me the tiny opening I needed to push forward. There was still a lot that was missing, a lot I couldn't explain, and maybe there was no Grodnik family secret beyond Iris's long-ago marriage, and if they were holding anything else back, it might have nothing whatever to do with the killing of Iris.

I got into New York before the time I estimated school would be out and found a place across the street from the Garganus home to wait. It's hard to be unobtrusive on a street that has few passersby and I find it easier to walk than to stand, so I kept moving around, standing only when motion sickness threatened. I had no idea whether Erin would come home in a taxi, a limousine, a car, or on foot. Was her grandmother nervous enough about her welfare to forbid her to walk? Of course, I didn't know what school she was coming from, and although there were some good private schools in the area, there were others a great enough distance away that she would need some kind of transportation.

But although plenty of cars went down the street, none stopped in front of the Garganus house, and when I was starting to think that Erin had stayed after school for sports or some other activity, she drifted down the block like a happy waif, her books in a canvas backpack that was probably the height of style but looked a little ratty to me. She walked slowly, half dreaming, and had I been closer, I would not have been surprised to hear her singing.

I crossed the street and walked towards her, but she seemed oblivious until we nearly collided.

"Hi, Erin," I said, "I'm Chris Bennett. I talked to you and your grandmother last week."

"Oh, hi. I remember. It was the day I was home sick."

"That's right. You just coming home from school?"

"Uh-huh. It's a nice day, isn't it?"

"Beautiful. How old are you, Erin?"

"Fifteen and a half. You live around here?"

"No. I just needed to ask your grandmother something. Can I come in with you?"

"Sure. She should be home. If not, she'll be back soon." We had reached the front door with its gleaming brass trim and she rang the bell.

The door was opened by a maid in uniform who smiled at Erin and looked questioningly at me.

"Hi, Elena. Grandma home?"

"She's upstairs."

"This is Chris. She has to see Gram. It's OK."

Elena's face showed that she didn't agree with my acceptability, but I scooted in and followed Erin up the beautiful stairs to the beautiful living room.

"Hi, Gram," Erin said, dashing lightly across the rug to where her grandmother sat reading. They kissed and Erin said, "Chris is here. She wants to talk to you again. I'm gonna do my homework so I can go to Jennifer's tonight and work on the language project."

Mrs. Garganus gave her a smile and then looked at me sourly. "We have nothing to talk about, Miss Bennett," she said when Erin had bounded up the stairs.

"I think we do. I think your husband saw Iris Grodnik the night she died."

"Miss Bennett, this is absurd. Miss Grodnik no

longer worked for GAR. What would my husband need to talk to her about?"

"You tell me."

"There is nothing to tell you because they had nothing to talk about." Her pretty face was grim and she touched a gold choker at her neck as though to reassure herself that it was still there.

"Erin's about fifteen and a half, isn't she?" I said.

Her face came alive. "What business is that of yours?"

"I think Erin and Iris Grodnik had a connection."

"That's ridiculous. Erin was born after Iris died. There is no connection."

"How does Erin come to have the name Garganus?"

"Because she's— Miss Bennett, this is not your business. If you don't leave, I'll call the police and have you removed."

"If you don't tell me the connection, if you don't tell me what your husband was doing on East Seventy-first Street the night that Iris disappeared, I will tell Detective Harris White what my suspicions are and he will reopen the investigation and center it on your husband."

She touched the gold again. I noticed she hadn't moved toward the bell that would summon the maid or the telephone that lay on a table many feet from her wheelchair. The last thing she wanted was the police, whether she called them or I did.

"You seem to have come to several erroneous conclusions," she said with forced composure.

"Iris was doing your husband a favor," I said. "She was doing both of you a favor. They met that night so that he could give her something. What was it, Mrs.

Garganus, money? Was it the key to an apartment where she would stay with someone?"

She looked a little paler. "You don't know what you're talking about. This is worse than conjecture; this is pure malicious fantasy."

"Did they argue about the amount? Did he drag her into his car and drive her somewhere? Was he alone in the car or did he have a driver who witnessed the whole thing?"

"This is nonsense, this is slander, and I don't have to listen to it." But she made no move. She sat perfectly still.

"Tell me what happened that night."

"I will not."

"But you know, don't you?"

"My husband was here with me. We heard about Iris's death after they found her body. That's all I know."

"What about your daughter?" I hadn't wanted to say it. The thought of her daughter must have been so painful that I had hoped not to have to bring the matter up. If she wanted to talk about it, it was her option.

"What about my daughter?" she said in a low, quivering voice.

"She was pregnant."

"Get out of here."

It had been Taffy's story to Eileen that had eventually made me think about it. Erin Garganus had been born after Iris died, enough afterward that Iris might have been the person chosen by the family to stay with their pregnant daughter. Perhaps she was suicidal even then, perhaps she wanted an abortion and the Garganuses could not condone it. But they could trust Iris. Iris could take their daughter to Europe, to Switzerland or wherever the parents wanted her to go, and she could stay with her till she gave birth. Then she could come back and resume her job, having taken a wonderful midlife sabbatical. She could talk to the old gossips in the office about the beauty of Switzerland, the charm of Paris, the rest and relaxation in Spain. But something had gone wrong the night of the seder, and instead of going to Europe, she had ended up dead among rusting trucks in the oil yards.

"Tell me, Mrs. Garganus. I will do everything I can to protect your privacy—and Erin's—and to protect what's dear to you."

"I have nothing to say."

"The Grodnik family wants to know what happened to their sister. Her oldest brother is dying now. Her sister cries every year at the Passover seder. Please tell me what you know."

"My husband didn't harm her."

"Then what was he doing there that night?" I was sure now that Wilfred Garganus had been the person Iris had gone downstairs to meet. I hadn't been sure when I walked inside this house with Erin, but I was now. Now I was certain that my vague suspicions were founded in truth. If I didn't know exactly what happened, I was close enough that Mrs. Garganus was afraid that I knew as much as she did.

"Take your coat off and sit down. I can't bear having you stand there." She turned her chair to face the sofa I sat on. "I have never told anyone what I know. The police interviewed my husband after they found Iris's body, and he told them the truth, or as much of it as he felt was necessary. He didn't know what happened to her, and since he wasn't involved, he felt it wasn't necessary to discuss family matters that had nothing to do with her murder."

"But I've come close," I said.

"Very close. Miss Bennett, I don't know who killed her. I tell you honestly, I don't know if my husband knew who the killer was, but I don't think he did and I didn't want to know. We had enough to worry about at that time in our own family." She wheeled herself a little closer. "Our daughter was a troubled child. We gave her everything, we did everything for her. No school had the right friends for her. No doctor was able to activate in her the strength of character I knew she was born with but which she was unable to summon when she needed it. She got mixed up with the wrong people, she drank alcohol at an age when I would not have considered it, she used drugs. She was our only child and we were desperate and unable to help her."

"I'm sorry. I understand how hard it must have been and how hard it must be now to talk about it."

She glanced at the staircase and turned back to me. Erin was in her room, the good student doing her homework. I hoped.

"She became pregnant about sixteen years ago, a little more. We found out who the boy was—the young man. They were both in their twenties. Take my word for it that he was worthless. I didn't want her to marry him any more than she wanted to. First she said she wanted the baby, then she said she didn't, and finally it was too late to make a decision. Nature had made it for her. She was too far along for an abortion. We talked about the baby and never came to a decision. Would she give birth and give it up or would she try to be a mother? I thought having a baby might turn her around, might give her a reason to stay sober and off drugs. If I was naive, I apologize. This was my only child and she was carrying what might be my only grandchild. But I did not want the world to know what was a private, family matter."

"You wanted her to go away to have the child."

"Precisely. But we couldn't let her go alone. I could have gone with her—I was up and about in those days—but there would have been too much explaining to do. I don't know when we thought of Iris, but the moment her name was mentioned, we knew she was the perfect person. She had no family responsibilities, we had known her for years, and Wilfred trusted her as much as if she had been a sister. And there was another thing," she said, cocking her head to the side. "She had a wonderful personality. She was a happy, upbeat person. She got along with people, and people liked her. Wilfred asked her one day at work. It was short notice because I wanted Pattie, that's our daughter, out of here before her condition became noticeable. I remember that Iris said she couldn't leave immediately. Her family was getting together for her holiday, Passover, I think it was. And one of the girls in the office was getting married and she had promised to go to the shower. But after that, she would be ready to go anywhere."

"So she pretended to quit her job."

"Yes. She left on a Friday and took a couple of weeks to put her affairs in order. She said there were people she had to see, plants in her apartment she had to give to friends who would care for them, clothes she had to buy. Of course, we paid for everything, you understand."

"She hadn't told her family anything about it," I said. "They didn't even know she had quit her job. The only person who knew was her oldest friend."

"I'm sure she would have taken care of all that the following week. I know that she had ordered her passport. It probably came after she died. And Wilfred booked airline tickets for her and Pattie and arranged for a place for them to stay in Switzerland. It was the tickets and the cash that he was giving her the night she was taken away."

"He gave her cash?"

"He didn't want a record of a lot of money going into her bank account. Wilfred was very concerned about appearances. If she was audited, how would she explain a large deposit? He gave her enough money to get them comfortably to where they were going and intended to send more along later. She was going to take the money and buy traveler's checks the next day, except she never did."

"Do you know how much he gave her?"

"I don't know for sure, but it was at least a thousand."

"So she had a thousand dollars and an airline ticket in her hand or her coat pocket."

"Probably in her purse."

"We found her purse last week in her brother's closet. It had been there for sixteen years hidden among boots and umbrellas. She went down to meet your husband without taking it with her."

"She intended to go back up, I suppose. She told him she would slip out for a few minutes and meet him downstairs."

"Did he walk or drive, Mrs. Garganus?"

"He walked. He used to enjoy a walk at night. When the weather was fair I would go with him. That night he went alone."

"What happened when he came home?"

"He was upset. He said Iris had been there, he had given her everything, but he was upset about something. He didn't want to tell me about it, I suppose to spare me anxiousness, but after Iris's body was found, he said that as he was leaving her, someone called her name."

"A man?"

"That was the impression I got. Whoever it was, he had a car nearby and Iris got into it."

"Did she struggle? Cry out? Argue?"

She looked pained. "It was Wilfred's feeling that she didn't want to go, but she didn't do any of the things you suggested. She got in the car, Wilfred waited for a minute or two, and saw the car drive away."

"Did he get a license plate number? A description?"

"Miss Bennett, he had no idea at the moment that the man was a killer. It was obviously someone she knew because he knew her name. In fact—wait a moment." She furrowed her forehead as though the wrinkle would extract the memory. "Wilfred said the man called her I."

"I? As in Iris?"

"Yes. He said, 'I? Iris?' That's how Wilfred repeated it to me. Anyway, by the time we heard she was dead, it was too late to think about a license plate or a description."

"He didn't tell the police any of this, did he?"

"I don't honestly know what he told the police, but I expect he didn't discuss any of it. What he went to see her for was our concern, not that of the police. And since he couldn't furnish any description of the man or the car, why should he mention it?"

I could think of some reasons, but it was sixteen years too late to make an issue of them and I didn't want to hurt this woman who had not herself been involved. "What happened to the airline tickets?" I asked.

"After her body was found, he canceled the reservations."

"I see."

"We made other arrangements for Pattie," she said, as though I needed to know the end of the story. "And when Erin was born, they came here to live. Eventually we adopted her."

"It seems to have worked out very well."

"Yes." She looked down. She had lost her daughter, but she had done her best. "So far I seem to have succeeded at motherhood much better the second time."

"I'm sure you succeeded the first time, Mrs. Garganus. A mother can't control everything in her daughter's life."

"Perhaps," she said with a small smile, "she can try a little harder."

24

Iris had met two men in the street that night, and she had known them both. Joseph was right; one of them had given her something. But the Grodnik family was just as correct; the other had taken something from her, eventually her life. Two men, and she had known them both. But had the meeting with both men been planned or had the second one been accidental? There was no notation for any meeting at all the night of the seder.

Perhaps, I thought, walking to my car from the Garganus town house, the arrangement to meet her boss had been made late, possibly just that afternoon over the telephone. And the second meeting, the one that ended her life, could have been a coincidence. It was even possible that the *M* who had planned to see her the night of the second seder had changed his mind and decided to drop by on the night of the first. And he had known where it would be and that Iris would be there.

I got my car and drove uptown, thinking about that and a few other things. Mrs. Garganus's mention of the passport had also caught my attention. When Marilyn's mother found it in the mail at Iris's apartment, it must have prompted a lot of discussion and questions in the family. Perhaps that was one of the papers Abraham had incinerated yesterday morning. What had they thought? I wondered. That Iris had planned to run away with someone? That she had retired without telling them and was moving to Europe? That she was going to visit the mythical son that apparently existed only in my imagination? Abraham Grodnik would never tell me and I could not ask.

I picked up the FDR Drive and drove up to the George Washington Bridge. I had Shirley Mandelbaum's address with me and a map of Bergen County. Jack was coming home late tonight, so it didn't matter when I got home, and if I could corner her, now that I had information from Mrs. Garganus, maybe she would tell me something more. I crossed the bridge and found my way to Teaneck. I had been here once before when I had investigated the first homicide of my amateur career, but I was going to a residential area this time, not a Catholic church. I made a few wrong turns and stopped to ask directions twice and then I was on a quiet street with lawns and trees and shrubs, not unlike the one I live on in Oakwood. Children were playing outside several houses, and three women with strollers stood at the curb talking as their toddlers looked around and chewed wetly on snacks.

The Mandelbaum house was at the far end of the street, one of several older houses built long before the group I was driving through. Here the trees were taller and thicker, the shrubs woven together in a natural fence, the houses stone. I parked at the curb and walked up a slate walk to the front door.

The woman who opened the door could have been a sister to Iris Grodnik. Small and very thin, she had a full head of gray hair and bright eyes that might still be looking for mischief.

"Mrs. Mandelbaum, I'm Chris Bennett. We spoke last night."

She shook her head. "You didn't have to make a big trip. Come in. I'll give you a cup of coffee, but there's nothing else I can tell you."

"I spoke to Mrs. Garganus today, just a little while ago. She told me about the trip Iris was going to make."

"She told you?"

"All of it." I took my coat off and she hung it in a closet. "About how her daughter was pregnant."

"I can't believe she told you. Can I get you some coffee?"

"No, thanks."

"Then let's sit in the living room. Harold's in the family room watching a thirty-year-old baseball game on cable." She smiled. "What is it with men? It happened thirty years ago and he sits and agonizes like it's happening now."

I couldn't help but like her. I sat in a chair in a living room that looked as though it didn't get much use. Everything was blue and puffy and had the undisturbed quality of a museum. Shirley sat in a hard chair, explaining that if she took the sofa, she'd never get out of it.

"Shirley?" a man's voice called. "Someone come in?" He appeared suddenly, an old man in corduroy pants and a flannel shirt.

"Go back to your game, Harold. This is the lady I told you about, who's trying to find out who killed my friend Iris. We'll talk a little and then I'll get your dinner. Go or you'll miss your ball game."

He greeted me and left. "Have you lived here long?" I asked.

"Almost thirty years. Harold was a widower with two kids. I was very lucky."

I was pretty sure they were even luckier. "No one even referred to you by your married name."

"No, I guess I'm Shirley Finster forever for the Grodniks."

"And you were Shirley Finster when you talked to the police."

"You know that, too."

"I've talked to the detective."

"There was nothing I could tell him. Why should I have a policeman on my doorstep? Chris, what can I tell you that could help you find Iris's killer?"

"I think you're the one who knows that."

"She was killed by a man who probably robbed her. How could I know who he was?"

"Because he knew her. The night Iris left the seder, Mr. Garganus met her outside her brother's house to give her money and the plane tickets to Europe. Mrs. Garganus told me this afternoon that her husband heard the other man call Iris by name."

"Oh." Her lively little face clouded. "You're not making this up?"

"No. Mr. Garganus should have told the police what he saw and heard, but he didn't want to have to talk about why he was meeting Iris that night. So he never told them he was there and that he saw Iris get into a car."

"My God. It was someone with a car?"

"Someone with a car and he knew her. Do you think it was Harry Schiff?"

"Harry? Never. Harry was crazy about her. He would never have hurt her."

"Was it a new boyfriend then? Someone who was very jealous and didn't want her going away to Europe for six or seven months?"

"Honey, if there was a new boyfriend, I never heard about him."

"Could it have been Martin Handleman, her ex-husband?" I asked, running out of possibilities.

"What, from 1939, that idiot she married? That's ridiculous. She never saw him again."

"Could it have been a son that she had by Handleman? A son who came back to her and wanted money from her?"

She shook her head, her face tight, her forehead creased. "She had no son. I'm telling you, she had no children."

I could see that something was now bothering her. It was as though with each suspect that she crossed off my list, we came closer to someone she did not want to name. "You know who it is, don't you?" I said.

"You're sure he called her name?"

"It's what Mr. Garganus told his wife."

"My God, I can't believe it."

"He called her I, Mrs. Mandelbaum. He said, 'I? Iris?' " I imitated Mrs. Garganus's imitation.

Shirley paled.

"Who was this man?" I asked.

She shook her head. "I don't have the right. Abe is still alive?"

"He's dying, but he's still alive."

"Go home, honey. Forget it. Pretend it never happened."

I got up, my head almost throbbing. There was something I had seen or heard and it hadn't registered. Someone had said something to me, but what? There were so many people who had talked to me, so many bits of information. My head cleared and I saw that I was standing opposite Shirley, who was watching me as though I might do something violent or at least discourteous. But I was just searching, back through the people and the places and the memories.

A loud shout went up from the family room. "Atta boy," Shirley's husband roared. "You can do it. All the way. They can't stop you."

She smiled and I thought of her husband cheering on a ballplayer whose bat had connected thirty years ago. And then I had it.

"What happened?" Shirley said, seeing the change in my face.

"I know who it was. There's something I have to check."

"Wait a minute. You don't have any idea—"

"But I do. He worked at the oil yards. Joseph was right."

"You've got me all confused."

"I'll call you, Mrs. Mandelbaum. Thank you. You've been a great help."

"Whatever you do," she said, taking my coat out of the closet, "don't tell them I told you."

The answering machine was flashing, but I didn't want to take the time to listen to messages. I called Marilyn.

"Chris," she said, "I've been thinking about you all day. You must have something to tell me."

"I do. I learned a lot this afternoon. Mrs. Garganus finally told me the whole story. Her husband is the person Iris went downstairs to see. He gave her something—I'll tell you about it another time—and he saw her get into a car and drive away with a man."

"And he never told the police?"

"She went willingly. It was someone she knew, someone who called her name, someone who called her *I*."

"*I* for Iris?"

"Yes. Do you know anyone who did that?"

"Not offhand. Mel said something like that when she was little, *I* or Ice, but I don't remember any of the adults saying it."

"Do you know where Iris was intending to go to the second seder?"

"Good question. Sixteen years ago I might have known. Usually my parents made the first one and they went somewhere else for the second. Maybe my brother that year. I think we were going to my in-laws'."

"Your brother Dave?"

"Yes. He's the oldest."

"What's his last name, Marilyn?"

"Gordon. Both my brothers changed their names."

My heart was absolutely thumping. I had met her youngest brother, Sandy, a few months ago and completely forgotten that his name was Gordon. "When you were outside the shack at the oil yards, the guard told me that a man named Gordon had worked there for a short time."

"Chris, neither of my brothers killed my Aunt Iris. Dave was at the seder and Sandy was with his wife's family. If Sandy hadn't been there, you can be sure his wife would have made a stink about it. She made a stink about everything else."

I knew that she and Sandy had eventually divorced. "I'm going to call the security guard and see if he remembers the first name of the Gordon who worked there."

"You'd better get back to me," Marilyn said, her voice without its usual firmness.

"I will."

I dialed the number in Manhattan, but there was no answer. A security guard has to make his rounds, I thought, and maybe this was one of those times. I cut a slice from the roast beef in the refrigerator, wrapped it in foil, and put it in the oven to heat. Then I opened a can of mixed vegetables, my way of seeing that I got a little of everything, and warmed it on the stove. A half grapefruit started me off and I read the morning paper while I ate it. Half an hour later, dishes done, I dialed Juan Castro once again.

"Security, Castro."

"Mr. Castro, this is Chris Bennett. We talked yesterday."

"Oh sure, about the woman's body."

"You said some people had worked for short periods of time as security guards."

"Right. Giordano was one of them."

"And there was a Gordon."

"Yeah, there was a Gordon. It was a long time ago."

"Do you remember about how old a man he was?"

"Not young. He could've been sixty." That was almost Iris's age.

"Do you remember anything about him?"

"A little. He'd been around, traveled. Said he'd come back to New York because he knew people here. He'd lived here when he was young. You know, it's not like an office here. You don't get to talk to a guy very much because he walks in as you're walking out. It's just a few words now and then. I was interested because he said he'd traveled. It's something I'd like to do myself."

"Do you remember his first name?"

"Oh boy." There was silence. "Uh, something like Morrow? Uh, Maurice? It's hard to remember. It's been a long time."

"Morrow or Maurice," I repeated.

"Something like that. Morris maybe. Yeah, I think that's it. Morris Gordon. The old brain's still working. Maybe I'll go for a Ph.D."

"I bet you'll get it, Mr. Castro. I can't thank you enough."

I put the phone down and looked at the name I had written on the back of an envelope. Morris Gordon. There wasn't any Morris Gordon that Marilyn knew about, so that had to mean there was one that she didn't know about. My eye fell on the blinking answering machine and I pushed the Play button.

"Hiya, Chrissie, this is Arnold. Got some very juicy news for you. Give me a call when you come in."

Arnold's paralegal had been going to dig up some marriage and birth certificates. I dialed his number at work and, not surprisingly, found that no one was there. I checked my book and found his home phone number.

Harriet answered. "Good timing," she said. "Himself just walked through the door bitching about something. I couldn't tell if it was the subway system or the legal system."

"It's both," Arnold's voice said. "Get my message?"

"Got a lot more than that, Arnold. Tell me what you know."

"Found her marriage license and the address Martin Handleman lived at when he married her, but the building's been razed and I don't have anything else on him. But we looked up your Iris Grodnik's birth certificate. Did you know she was part of a multiple birth?"

"She had a twin?"

"Looks like it. We called the hospital, where they keep all those little details forever. Morris and Iris Grodnik were born of the same mother on the date you gave us."

"It had to be a brother," I said. "Arnold, you're wonderful."

"Well, I wouldn't go quite that far. Thank the City of New York for keeping good records. Is he your killer?"

"I think so. I don't even know if he's still alive, but I'll pass all this along to the detective."

"If he killed, there may be a file on him."

"I doubt he got into much criminal type trouble. He once worked as a security guard at the oil yards where the body was found. They would have checked up on him."

"Not the way you think. Till recently they've been pretty lax on background. Half the crimes in New York are committed by security guards," Arnold said with typical exaggeration. "But you made a connection the cops didn't. Make sure you point out their failings when you call your detective."

I laughed. "He's a very nice person and he was a brand-new detective when he caught that case. You'll be glad to hear it was Sister Joseph who made the connection for me. She said if she'd killed someone, she'd have dumped the body in Central Park."

"Woman's as sharp as they come. Give her my best. I'll send you a copy of the birth and marriage certificates tomorrow. Now I have to eat."

I had one more call to make, to Harris White at the Thirty-fourth Precinct. He wasn't there, and I decided quite suddenly not to leave my name for him. Maybe I could do this another way. I pulled out our collection of phone books and started looking up Gordons in Queens. There were lots of *M*s, many of them probably women, and three Morrises. One was an M.D., which left him out. I called the second and spoke to a woman whose husband had died thirteen years ago. Then I called the third.

"Hello?" It was a man's voice, elderly.

"Is this Morris Gordon?"

"Yeah. Who's this?"

"Shirley Finster gave me your name."

"Who?"

"Shirley Finster. Iris's friend. You remember Shirley."

I could hear him breathing. "You say Iris?"

"Yes. Iris Grodnik."

"Who is this?"

"I'm a friend of the family."

"I don't know what you're talking about." He hung up.

My heart was going a mile a minute.

25

"How can you get out of bed with such enthusiasm when it feels like the middle of the night?" Jack turned over with a groan.

It was 5:00 A.M. "When you've done it for fifteen years, it's part of you forever. Don't go back to sleep or I'll be forced to use very unpleasant means to get you up."

"You thinking of pulling out my fingernails one by one?"

"I'll deprive you of coffee." I was throwing clothes on as I spoke.

"Anything but that." He sat and stretched. "We really are going to do this?"

"You bet. I'll get breakfast."

We had talked about it last night and he had grudgingly agreed to drive to Queens with me early enough that he would get to the Sixty-fifth by ten, the time his tour of duty starts. Before talking to Harris White, I decided I wanted to see for myself what Morris Gordon looked like, sounded like, acted like. We were out of the house before six.

Fortunately, Jack knows his way around New York as if he has lived in every remote corner of every borough, which he hasn't. We went in two cars so we could leave in separate directions. When Jack finally put his turn signal on and pulled over to the curb, I got a case of serious butterflies. We had arrived.

The street was filled with old houses with barely space for a narrow prewar driveway between them. Some were New York–style semiattached, some were one-family with an occasional front porch. All had tiny lawns or the concrete that replaced what had once been a small rectangle of grass. I got out as Jack did.

"Across the street," he said.

It was one of the single-family houses, an unlikely place for Morris Gordon, I thought, unless the house had been converted. We walked up to the front door and Jack rang.

A sleepy-looking woman in a bathrobe opened it and looked blankly at us.

"We're looking for Morris Gordon," Jack said.

"Can't you people wait till sunrise?" she said irritably. "The door on the driveway. He lives in the basement."

Jack thanked her and we walked around the corner of the house. The door was at street level, and a few windows looked out on the driveway. Jack pressed the doorbell and we heard a loud buzz inside.

"I'm a little nervous," I admitted. "But I want to do the talking."

"Let's see if he's there first."

He was. The door was opened by an old man with sparse gray hair, wearing a navy blue terry cloth bathrobe, a two-day growth of beard darkening his face. He looked at us without saying anything.

"Mr. Gordon?" I said.

"What is this?"

"I'm Christine Bennett, Mr. Gordon. We spoke on the phone last night."

"Who's he?"

"My husband, Jack Brooks. May we talk to you?"

"What's this about?" His eyes darted fearfully from my face to Jack's.

"Iris."

"You a cop?" he said to Jack.

"Yes, I am." Jack took his shield out, but Morris Gordon barely glanced at it.

He opened the door and we followed him down half a flight of stairs. "Took you guys a hell of a long time," he said. "How many years is it now?"

"Sixteen," I said.

"Sit down."

Jack stayed near the door, and I found a place to sit on an old wing chair. Morris Gordon sat on a sofa and lit a cigarette. There were ashtrays everywhere, most of them overflowing.

"I don't get it. What are you doing here?" he asked me.

"I'm a friend of Iris's niece. She asked me to look into her murder."

He smiled and shook his head. "*You* found me?"

"I found you. One of the security guards at the oil yards remembered you."

"The good-looking one with the Spanish name."

"What happened, Mr. Gordon? Why did you do it?"

"I don't remember anymore. It was a long time ago." He blew smoke. His face was pale, as though he didn't get out much. He was a small man, hardly as tall as I. Even when he sat he looked small.

"It was Passover," I prompted him. "You drove over to your brother's apartment."

"Why not? I was part of the family, wasn't I?"

"What happened with Iris?"

"She was trying to cut me off. I was just getting back on my feet. I had a job, she knew that, and I had debts. She was helping me out, but she told me it had to stop. It couldn't go on forever, that's what she said. Then she made up this cock-and-bull story that she had to go away, her boss was sending her to Switzerland for six months, she couldn't help me anymore. Did she think I was stupid? She was a secretary. Secretaries don't get sent to Switzerland by their bosses. She was going to see me the next day, give me a little something, and that would be it." He stubbed out the cigarette and fished around for another. "Like a parting gift." After sixteen years it still made him angry to think about it.

I didn't say anything. The old feelings were building in him, the memory of that time, of that night, resurfacing. I wanted them to break through so that the truth would burst out.

"So I drove over to my brother's. I hadn't seen him in what? Forty years or more? He was my brother. It was a holiday. It was a good night to drop in and see the family."

And try to get on better terms with them so someone else would help him with his debts if Iris wouldn't. He was a conniver, but on that night something had gone wrong.

"I parked right near the building and I saw her come out of the front door. I was going to call her, but she walked over to a big guy who was standing there, waiting for her, a big, handsome guy. I could see even at night he was like a movie star. They talked for a minute and he pulled something out of his pocket, like an envelope or something, and gave it to her. Then they talked a little more and she left him and walked back to the door. So I called her and she came over to the car." He had lit another cigarette and now he drew on it and exhaled a cloud of smoke. "I just wanted to talk to her," he said with a whine in his voice. "I asked her what was in the envelope and she said it was nothing and I grabbed it from her and looked inside."

He looked at me and I looked back, feeling almost breathless.

"You know what she had?" he said. "It was like a thousand bucks. More. This guy is giving her envelopes of cash and she can't help her brother out a little?" The anger was fresh and new again. "I drove somewhere, I don't even remember where. We were fighting the whole time, shouting at each other. My own sister trying to cut me off." He drew on the cigarette. "So I hit her."

Jack stirred for the first time, moving closer to where we were sitting. "I have to warn you, Mr. Gordon," he said. "You have the right to remain silent. You—"

"Forget the TV," Morris Gordon said, waving Jack away. "I know my rights. I said it and you heard it. It's done." He leaned back on the sofa and smoked, but muscles in his face moved and the hand holding the cigarette shook slightly.

I swallowed hard. "You must have been very angry."

He shook his head. "My own sister." He looked at Jack. "You gonna take me in?"

"Yes, sir," Jack said. "You can put some clothes on first."

Morris tamped out the cigarette and went into the bedroom. I found the phone and called Harris White.

"Chris. What a morning," Harris White greeted me as I reached his desk. It was hours since Jack and I had walked into Morris Gordon's basement apartment in Queens, and he was now being held at the station house in his precinct.

"You can say that again."

"I can't believe it. I swear I checked out everything."

"A lawyer I know got Iris's birth certificate and talked to the hospital where she was born. That's how I found out about the twin. I found his address in the Queens phone book."

"I did some digging after you called. Gordon's been living there seventeen years."

"So he'd been there a year when Iris died."

"And he'd spent six months of that year as a night watchman at the oil yards. It's all falling into place. I'll be going over to Queens this afternoon to interview him, but I gather he's made a pretty full statement. You want to fill me in on what you know?"

"Sure."

"Let's have lunch. My treat."

"I'd love to."

I told him what had happened that morning and everything else I thought would be helpful. Although Wilfred Garganus was long dead, I described what had happened between Wilfred and Iris to explain Morris's motivation, and Harris promised to keep confidential what the Garganuses preferred not to become public. By the end of our lunch he was showing me pictures of his children, and I was asking his advice on building a family room.

I drove home, knowing I would have to tell Marilyn everything and feeling squeamish about it. An uncle she had never known existed was alive and well and being questioned by the police for the murder of her aunt. Somehow it wasn't the stuff of a friendly conversation.

There were two messages on the machine when I got home. The first was from Eileen asking me to call back. The second was from Mel and she sounded funny. I called her right away.

"Oh, Chris," she said, her voice weary, "Grandpa died last night."

"I'm so sorry," I said, the information making a ripple through my body. "I hope he wasn't in pain."

"I don't think he was. Mrs. Hires found him this morning. He died in his sleep. The funeral will be tomorrow."

"I'd like to go."

"You can follow us in your car. We'll be going on to the cemetery. I don't think you'll want to do that. Come by at nine."

"I will. Will you be home today?"

"Sure. Mom's taking care of the arrangements and then I think she'll pick up Aunt Sylvie. She shouldn't be alone. It's her last brother."

I didn't comment. "I'll pick up some dinner for you, Mel. I'll drop it off later this afternoon."

"Oh, Chris, what a lovely thing to do."

"I learned about it from good people," I said.

I drove over to the kosher delicatessen that Mel had introduced me to and bought a little of this and a little of that the way she did. The salads looked wonderful, and their rye bread with seeds had a smell that would drive you crazy. I left with so many things that I needed a shopping bag.

Mel looked pretty washed out when she opened the door, and when she hugged me, we both cried.

"Stay for a while," she said. "Hal's gone to pick up Sylvie, and I'd love to talk about something else. It's so sad. He wanted to see the flowers bloom."

"Some of the trees have started to leaf out. He probably saw them yesterday."

"I hope so." She got up and went to the window. "You're right. The willow is green and there are some green buds on the other trees. Maybe he did see them. Maybe it was enough."

We talked for a while, but it wasn't about other things. Finally I said I'd see her in the morning.

"Stay for dinner," she said.

"I don't think so. There are some things I have to work out."

"I forgot. You've been looking into Aunt Iris's death."

"We'll talk about it another time."

I went home and called Eileen. She wanted to set up a time to meet with Taffy. I told her Friday would be fine and we left it at that. Then I called Shirley Finster.

"In custody?" Shirley said. "You got Morris Gordon in custody?"

"He killed Iris. I talked to him this morning myself."

"Oh my God."

"Did anyone in Marilyn's generation ever know that Aunt Iris had a twin brother?"

"Nobody. Not one person. He quit school when he was a kid. He was a troublemaker, not big trouble, just enough that he was hard to get along with. Nowadays they would say he has low self-esteem. Back then it was an inferiority complex. He thought everyone in the family got better than he did."

"Did you know him, Shirley?"

"Sure I knew him. They went to the same school as me. Then one day something happened, a big fight with his parents, and he left. We're talking sixty years ago, the nineteen thirties. It was the Depression. Maybe he had a dollar or two in his pocket, maybe less. Iris was a wreck. Whatever happened, she loved him. I never saw him again after that."

"But Iris did."

She took a deep breath. "She didn't talk about it much, but I think he called her sometimes or wrote her a letter."

"She was giving him money," I said.

"I'm not surprised."

"Why didn't he go to his brothers or his other sisters?"

"What, and say, 'Look, here I am after forty years. Can you give me some money now that I'm back?' This man wasn't even there when his parents died. He never called to see how anyone was, if they were sick, if he could do anything for them. You heard of the black sheep in the family? Morris was the original black sheep."

"Before the night of the seder she told him she wouldn't give him any more money, that she was going to Switzerland and that was the end."

"No," Shirley said. "It wasn't the end. For Iris there was never any end."

"I guess Morris didn't understand that."

"Then he was the only one, let me tell you."

26

The funeral was short, and the room in the funeral home where it took place, very bare. Like the only other Jewish funeral I had attended, there were no flowers. The casket, made of a lustrous wood, was front and center but largely ignored. A rabbi spoke for several minutes about the life and family of Abraham Grodnik and then Marilyn's older brother gave a short eulogy that came from the heart and was delivered with great difficulty. After a few closing remarks from the rabbi, it was over.

I had signed the book and spoken to every member of the family whom I knew, so I slipped away quickly and drove back to Oakwood. Waiting on my answering machine was a message from Harris White. I called him back right away.

"We've got what we need," Harris said right off the bat. "He made a full confession."

I felt a pang of guilt. I should have told Marilyn. Maybe someone in the family would have gotten him a lawyer. "Is it substantially what he told me?"

"Not quite, but it's good enough. Of course, he didn't mean to do it. He was going to his brother's apartment to see his family for the first time in over forty years.

But when he got there, his sister walked out of the front door and met someone. He watched, he saw the guy give her something and then walk away. He said he was planning to meet her the following afternoon in Queens. He never really admitted to us that she gave him money—I guess the guy still has some pride—but he said they got into a fight, he hit her, she died, and he had to dump the body. You and I know it was a lot more than that, Chris. He really bloodied her."

"And he stole her money and the airline tickets."

"Right. He's a little fuzzy on some details like that, but thanks to his openness, we really have a case."

"Harris, his oldest brother died yesterday. I went to the funeral this morning. I want to talk to someone in the family about this. I don't know what they'll do, if anything, but this is a very difficult time."

"I understand. But I've got to turn what I've got over to the DA, and there'll be an arraignment. If you think someone's going to spring for a lawyer, I'd say the sooner the better."

"I'll take care of it."

It was late when the Grosses returned home. I guessed they must have gone to Marilyn's house after the cemetery. I waited so that Mel would have time to relax after the ordeal of this long day. Then I walked down the block and rang her doorbell.

"Come on in," she said. "What a day. We were at Mom's till the kids couldn't take it anymore. I brought home some cake. Hal and I are just sitting with our feet up and munching. Join us."

We talked for a few minutes about who had come,

how far they had traveled, how many friends Abraham Grodnik had had, even at his advanced age.

Then I said, "Mel, there's something that can't wait. It's about Iris. We have her killer."

They both listened with shock and undivided interest. I left a lot out, but I made my point. Iris's twin brother was in custody. When I finished, Mel said, "Hal, I hate to do this to you, but would you take Chris to Mom's so she can make a decision? I think Chris is right. It can't wait."

I protested that I could go myself, but Hal put his shoes back on and we got in his car and drove. Marilyn Margulies's house, a twenty-minute ride from Oakwood, was all lit up and had cars parked up and down the block. We went in the open front door and found Marilyn in the living room talking to relatives. She gave us an odd look as she saw us and came over.

"Chris has something that's going to blow your mind," Hal said. "Tell her."

Marilyn is a cool woman. She can handle catastrophes as though they were ordinary mishaps. But my story left her reeling. She kept asking me to repeat things, to explain things I hadn't wanted to mention until a later time, but which she needed in order to understand the whole story. Finally she said, "Where is he?"

"I'm not sure. He was taken to a precinct in Queens yesterday morning, but by now he's probably been taken downtown to be booked at 100 Centre Street, the courts. I don't know where he's spending the night, but I would guess he'll end up at Rikers in the next day or so."

She paled. "Does he have a lawyer?"

"They'll get him one."

She considered this. "He needs a lawyer, doesn't he?" she asked Hal.

"He'd be better off with a good lawyer."

"Do you know one?"

"Are you sure you want to do this?"

She looked as though she wasn't. "He's my father's brother," she said. "If he's admitted his guilt, he'll probably be convicted anyway, but maybe a good lawyer can make it easier for him. I think we should get one for him. He's family."

Hal dropped me off at my house, and I ate half the Care package Marilyn had insisted I take home with me. Later, Jack finished it with gusto while I told him my story. With all the talk it was a late night for us. The only thing I didn't tell him was that his sister was coming up the next day to have her face-to-face with Taffy.

Eileen was bringing lunch, so there was nothing for me to do except blow away the dust and organize the living room. When I was done with that, I went into the dining room to put the papers on the table in some kind of order. That was when I saw it.

There was a separate small pile of papers at one end of the table with a note in Jack's hand on top. "Chris honey, Look this stuff over and let's talk. Jack."

I pulled out a chair and sat down. There were estimates for a family room, a family room with a bedroom above it, both with a bathroom. There were also little handwritten notes from people whose names were vaguely familiar, one agreeing to help frame the rooms, one to do the tile work, one to do the wiring. I looked at all of it with awe. The bottom sheets were forms from a bank and they described a loan that would cover the construction. When I see numbers in five figures, I have a tendency to palpitate. Then I looked at what the monthly payments would be, and they looked a lot less formidable than I had anticipated. Two signatures were required. Jack had already signed on one line.

OK, I thought. You promised to love and honor him forever. This is the other shoe dropping. Do it, Kix. Do it while you've got the nerve.

I signed.

Eileen arrived before noon, a large package held carefully in two hands. I took it from her and she gave me her famous grin.

"I'm scared you-know-whatless," she said. "Thanks for giving us neutral ground to dance around in. By the way, the packages marked 'lunch' should be heated. The rest are for you and Jack whenever."

"You're too good to us, Eileen," I said, taking the box into the kitchen and beginning to sort things out.

"Does my brother know we're doing this today?"

"I haven't breathed a word. He wants you to press charges and never see Taffy again outside a courtroom."

"I won't do that—press charges. There's too much history between us. But I think I've got down what I'm going to say and what I'm not going to say."

I didn't ask her anything else. Our plan was to eat lunch first. Taffy was expected at one, and I was going to keep out of sight unless called, which I dearly hoped would not happen.

When the timer rang, Eileen took everything out of the oven and we arranged things on the table. This meal was fish, fillets of sole rolled around a wonderful filling of mushrooms and other good things, and cooked in white wine. There were Eileen's usual marvelous vegetables and rice with the kinds of flavors I appreciate but have no idea how to generate myself. And there was a loaf of fresh-baked bread that she had picked up this morning from the special baker she always used for her jobs.

We talked about everything except Taffy while we ate. I told her Jack's plans for the family room plus and she agreed it was a fabulous idea, that it would make the house different and special while keeping it essentially the same, whatever that meant.

We got the dishes done well before one and I set up the coffeemaker, ready to push the button when the doorbell rang. By the time it was one, I was almost as nervous as my sister-in-law.

"Just stay with me until she comes, OK?" Eileen said as we left the kitchen.

"Sure."

"Where will you be? Upstairs? In the kitchen?"

"I can be either place. In the kitchen I'll hear everything. Upstairs I won't. I'm happy in either place."

"I'll think about it," Eileen said, looking at her watch again. "When she gets here, I'll make up my mind. I hope." She grinned. "I can't believe this is happening. I can't believe I'm so scared."

"Just remember, you've done nothing wrong and you have nothing to apologize for. Whatever you decide, we'll back you up. And that goes for Jack."

She stood and looked out the window at one-fifteen. The street, as usual, was empty. It was too early in the afternoon for kids on bicycles, and Pine Brook Road leads nowhere, so it isn't used as a shortcut or conduit.

It's a sleepy street in a sleepy town, and that's the way we all like it.

At twenty-five after I said, "Did you tell her how long it would take to get here?"

"To the minute. And my directions were perfect. There's no traffic at midday. She must have just left late. Damn."

I felt her anger and frustration. It was as though Taffy, having the upper hand, wanted to keep control by making all the rules and then breaking them to suit herself.

At twenty-five to two Eileen said, "Maybe I should call."

"Don't," I said. "She has this number. She has this address. Don't give her the satisfaction."

"You're right."

"Shall I put the coffee on? We really don't have to wait."

"Good idea." She went toward the kitchen. "I'll do it."

The aroma drifted into the living room and I went to pour, checking the front window first. There was no sign of Taffy. Eileen followed me to the kitchen.

"I'll cut the cake. I hope you like it. You didn't have much lunch. I have an excuse, but you don't."

"Maybe I'm just as nervous as you."

We carried cups and cake plates back to the living room and sat. The phone rang and I jumped, looked at Eileen as though to ask whether to answer my own telephone, and then went to the kitchen to answer.

"Chris, it's Marilyn."

"Hi, Marilyn. How's it going?"

"We're expecting people again this afternoon for a

while and then we'll take a break till Sunday. Hal got an attorney for—" she hesitated "—my uncle."

"That's very kind of you."

"It sounds as though he made such a full confession, there's not very much the lawyer can do, but maybe he can have Morris put away somewhere instead of going to prison. He's an old man and I don't think his health is very good. From what I hear, he hasn't done much to keep it."

"I appreciate your calling. I'm sorry I had to burst in on you yesterday with this."

"You did the right thing," Marilyn said. "It was urgent. We'll get together after a bit and sit down and you'll tell me the whole story."

I promised I would and went back to the living room. It was almost two.

"I don't know what to think," Eileen said. "Is she being mean or did she get lost or did she have a change of heart?"

"She didn't get lost."

"No, I guess not."

We sat until two-fifteen. Then Eileen stood. "I think I've gotten the message," she said, looking almost ready to break into tears.

"Why don't we take a walk? We can keep an eye on the house. If she shows up, we'll just dash back."

"That sounds good." She went to the coat closet and took out her coat while I went for my keys.

Outside it was sunny and cool but milder than it had been. Spring was really here. Down the block the willow near the Grosses' was bright green. We walked slowly and I started to talk about Iris Grodnik. Eileen kept looking back toward the house, but she was fascinated by the story and kept asking questions. At the far corner, we turned and slowly made our way back. When we reached the house it was past two-thirty.

"That's it," Eileen said. "She's not coming. It's over. She'll never know what I was going to say. I'm going to set up a new partnership with Mom."

"Eileen, that's a great idea."

"Mom's always helped out when we needed her and refused to take anything for it. Now she can be a full partner. When she decides to retire, I'll make another decision. But that's a long way away."

"I love it," I said. "And I bet your mom will, too."

"It'll work out because I have my own place. I don't think I could work with her all day and go home with her every night. But this is the perfect arrangement. Do me a favor, Chris. Don't tell my brother about today. He's always right, and sometimes it just kills me."

"He's not always right," I said, trying to keep a straight face. "I remember about six months ago he made a mistake about something. It was small, but it was a mistake."

Eileen giggled like a child.

"You know," I said, "I really owe your friend Taffy a debt. I was thinking of her and her sister's problem the other day when I was working on the Iris Grodnik murder, and it put me onto something that was very important. Although you didn't say so in so many words, I knew Taffy's sister was pregnant—I assume Taffy was setting her up somewhere to wait for the baby—and that made me think that Iris's boss's daughter might have been pregnant, too, kind of the same story sixteen years later."

"Taffy's sister isn't pregnant." Eileen looked at me with confusion in her eyes.

"She isn't?"

"Not that I know about. She gambled. She had huge debts and someone was threatening her if she didn't pay up right away."

"I can't believe it," I said. "From the moment you told me the story, I was sure that was it."

"Sorry. I didn't mean to mislead you, but that's the way it was."

It was my turn to laugh. "What a lucky misunderstanding," I said. "I have an idea. Let's go for a ride. I haven't seen my cousin Gene for a long time. I'll bring him a piece of cake."

Eileen put her arm around my shoulders and squeezed. "You're great," she said.

I almost cried.

27

Over the weekend we decided we would break ground as soon as we could line up a builder. To celebrate, we went out to dinner at Ivy's. Jack had their lobster special and I ordered the house chef salad.

"For dinner?" Jack said. "That's a lunch. They put that on the menu for those women who eat celery sticks. Are you OK?"

"I'm fine. I'm not very hungry."

"You look like hell."

"I do?"

"You've lost weight. I don't like the way you're eating. Are you pregnant?"

It stopped me for a moment. "I guess maybe I am. You think that's why I have no appetite?"

"Could be."

"How come you know about this and I don't?"

"I eavesdropped when I was growing up. Eileen said you didn't eat much yesterday."

"Eileen told you she was here?"

"Yeah. Why not?"

"I don't know. I thought she wanted to keep it a secret."

"Why would she do that?"

"I don't know. I guess I misunderstood. We had lunch together. Maybe I didn't eat as much as I usually do."

"She and Mom are going to be partners. What makes me think you know this already?"

"I think it's a great idea. She told me yesterday when she came for lunch."

His raised eyebrows told me he suspected something, but he didn't ask. "So Mom's going to be a partner and a grandmother. That's terrific."

"You're going to be a father, John Brooks."

"I guess I am." He gave me the smile that was half the reason I'd married him. "We did it, didn't we?"

"We really did."

"Have you been to a doctor yet?"

"Not yet. I guess I'll go pretty soon."

He leaned over and kissed me. "You want me to go with you the first time?"

"You really are a sweetheart. I don't think so, honey. I think I can handle it. Just be there at the end."

"I wouldn't miss it for the world."

It was a couple of weeks later, when the trees were leafing out in earnest, that Marilyn called and invited Mel and me to lunch at her house. It was one of those moments when I understood why women wanted to own silver and china and crystal. Marilyn had it all out on the dining room table as though we were royalty, or foreign dignitaries at the very least. And of course, the food was divine.

"Pop told me after the seder he was glad he'd met you, Chris," Marilyn said. "And he thought it was a wonderful joke that Jack walked in off the street like Elijah."

"I think it's what Morris Gordon wanted to do sixteen years ago."

"That's a very sad case. I think the lawyer's going to see that he never goes to trial."

"How do you feel about that?" I asked.

"I'm not bloodthirsty. We've found out what happened to Iris, and Morris has suffered a great deal because of it. From what I've learned, she paid his debts when he couldn't manage them. I think he bet on horses. She was as good-hearted as we all thought she was. And that counts for a lot. Sylvie's gone to see him in jail."

"It must be very hard for her."

"It is, but she's tougher than she looks. She told me that when she and my mother cleaned up Iris's apartment they came across letters Morris had written to Iris. Pop didn't want any of us kids to know about him. He was bad, he was gone, he didn't exist. It may sound harsh, but that was how he lived. They got rid of everything sixteen years ago, and what was left, if anything, he had Mrs. Hires incinerate the day we went to talk to him."

"So we might never have known if we hadn't gone to the oil yards and talked to Juan Castro."

Marilyn smiled. "Pop was smart, but he forgot one thing." She got up from the table and opened a drawer in her credenza. She came back with a black book with red-tinged pages. "This is the family Bible that Pop inherited when his parents died. Look." She opened it to a page near the center and handed it to me.

It was the list of family members, starting with names

I had never heard of, continuing to Abraham and then, in order of birth, the rest of the brothers and sisters. A few lines down were Iris and Morris.

"So even if you hadn't asked me to look into Iris's death, you would have opened this Bible just about now and seen the name," I said.

"What a shock that would have been," Mel said. "Discovering you had an uncle you'd never seen or heard of."

"Maybe less of a shock than the way it actually happened," her mother said. "But I would never have made the connection between him and Iris's murder. And I wouldn't have known where to look for him. It's been quite an experience."

"For all of us," I said. I gave the Bible back to Marilyn and watched as she put it back in the drawer. Then something dawned on me. "Did you find your father's poems?" I asked.

"What poems?"

"He told me when he was young he knew he wanted to be poet. He said that he had a whole boxful of poems in his apartment."

We looked at each other as the truth dawned on each one of us.

"He incinerated them," Marilyn said. "My father threw away his poems."

"He didn't want anyone reading them," Mel said. "He didn't want us to pass judgment."

"That's why he didn't want anyone looking around his home when he wasn't there," I said. "It wasn't evidence of Morris he was hiding; it was his poetry. He'd gotten rid of the other things sixteen years ago."

Marilyn shook her head. "He was proud up to the last

minute, wasn't he? What a man. What a wonderful man he was."

Spring came with the burst of color that I love. The loan was approved, a tentative date was set up for our addition, and I had seen an obstetrician for the first time when I picked up the Haggadah that Mel had given me to keep after the seder.

I sat in the backyard one afternoon and leafed through it, right to left, looking down the pages for something I remembered and wanted to read again. There were four sons, the wise, the wicked, the simple, and the one who was unable to ask a question. I wondered how Morris Gordon would be described. Surely not a wise son and perhaps too obviously a wicked one. But possibly neither of those characterizations was accurate. Perhaps he was simple, too simple to know right from wrong, too simple to do what was right.

I looked down at the English translation. Maybe all three were wrong. Maybe Morris's burden was that he was unable to ask a question, unable to pick up a phone and say, Abe? This is Morris. I know it's been a long time, but could I come home for Passover?

I was pretty sure I knew what the answer would have been.

A man of the cloth...
a bride of Christ...
a private detective???

Here's a heavenly assortment of mysteries featuring clergy who are also detectives....

THE CHRISTINE BENNETT MYSTERIES
by Lee Harris

Christine Bennett has left the cloistered world of nuns for the profane world of New York State.

———◆———

THE FATHER KOESLER MYSTERIES
by William X. Kienzle

Father Koesler is a reluctant—albeit intrepid— sleuth in Detroit.

———◆———

THE RABBI SMALL MYSTERIES
by Harry Kemelman

Murder always finds a way to distract David Small from his rabbinical duties.

———◆———

THE SISTER JOAN MYSTERIES
by Veronica Black

Sister Joan has found an additional calling to the one from above.

———◆———

Holidays can be murder.

THE GOOD FRIDAY MURDER
THE YOM KIPPUR MURDER
THE CHRISTENING DAY MURDER
THE ST. PATRICK'S DAY MURDER
THE CHRISTMAS NIGHT MURDER
THE THANKSGIVING DAY MURDER
THE PASSOVER MURDER
THE VALENTINE'S DAY MURDER

The Christine Bennett mysteries

by

Lee Harris

Published by Fawcett Books.
Available in bookstores everywhere.

Look for these novels by

LEE HARRIS

in your local bookstore.

Published by Fawcett Books.